Woven

*'If he owns so much land in this country,
why does he need more in Jamaica?'*

Angharad Tomos

Translated into English by Mícheál Ó hAodha

Gwasg Carreg Gwalch

First published in Welsh, *Y Castell Siwgr*, 2020
Published in English: 2022
© text: Angharad Tomos 2020
© English translation: Mícheál Ó hAodha 2022

ISBN: 978-1-84527-837-3

ebook ISBN: 978-1-84524-473-6

CYNGOR LLYFRAU CYMRU
BOOKS COUNCIL of WALES

Published with the financial support of the Books Council of Wales

Cover design: Hedydd Ioan

Map copyright:
Archive and Special Collections, Bangor University, Bangor Mss,
Penrhyn Castle Papers, Penrhyn Castle Additional Manuscripts/2787.

Published by Gwasg Carreg Gwalch,
12 Iard yr Orsaf, Llanrwst, Wales LL26 0EH.
tel: 01492 642031
email: books@carreg-gwalch.cymru
website: www.carreg-gwalch.cymru

Printed and published in Wales

To my sister Caitriona (RIP)
Ar dheis Dé go raibh sí.

Mícheál Ó hAodha

I would like to thank Llenyddiaeth Cymru
for the grant to write the book,
also Lois Mai, Bob Morris, Bethan Thomas, John Llywelyn Williams,
Ieuan Wyn, Liz Millman, Chris Evans, Manon Steffan Ros,
Gwyn Sion Ifan, Marian Gwynn, Gareth Evans-Jones,
Hanna Huws, Rhiannon Ifans, Lois Prys, Llio Elenid
and Gwynedd Library Service.

"I do not wish the cattle or the Negroes to be overworked."

Richard Pennant, Lord Penrhyn

Chapter 1

She let her body sway to the song's music, her feet beat to the tune. Dorcas was in her element – she was dancing.

> "Hwp dyna fo
> A chynffon buwch, a chynffon llo,
> A chynffon Rhisiart Parry'r Go,
> Hwp dyna fo ..." [1]

Holding hands to form a wide circle, she danced inwards with the others towards the maypole, watching in delight as its coloured ribbons wove into each other. Why couldn't every day be a holiday?

As the sound of the fiddle soared yet faster and higher, all of them dancing to the same beat, the dancers and the dance became one. Everyone woven together, winking, smiling, laughing. Nothing made Dorcas happier than dancing.

"Hey!"

Hefin Tŷ Uchaf squeezed Dorcas's waist and stole a quick kiss before hopping back into line. If only he'd been Rhys, she thought. Now that would have been a different story.

"Dorcas! Over here!"

The maydance was over, but a gang of them had formed a long line and, snakelike, they danced between the stalls –

[1] A Welsh verse which accompanied a popular May dance.

causing much merriment to all but the stallholders as their colourful kerchiefs and skirts darted like birds through the air.

"Give us a song!" someone shouted, and the fun continued as a voice obliged.

"Did you enjoy that?" Dorcas asked, turning breathlessly to her friend.

"Of course I did, even if it was nearly too much for me!"

Elsi was a small round dumpling of a girl, and her cheeks were as red as apples.

"Would you listen to you, Elsi! Don't worry – we'll have you up and dancing again before you know it."

"It didn't knock a stir out of you, did it, Dorcas?" asked Elsi in admiration.

No it didn't, thought Dorcas. I was made for this. I've a restless, lively soul and I'd love nothing better than to dance and sing all night long.

"If there was a competition for who could dance the longest, Dorcas would win it hands down," said Sara, and everyone laughed in agreement.

Then Rhys Fychan appeared, with a jug of water to quench their thirst. He smiled at Dorcas.

"I enjoyed watching you dance," he said, and Dorcas blushed from ear to ear.

"Thank you," she answered, unable to look him in the eye.

Collapsing on to the grass, the friends watched the bustle of the fair.

Lisa lay on her back, her head in Dorcas's lap, and Dorcas began braiding her hair – hair that was as blonde as broom-flowers.

"What are you up to, Dorcas?" asked Lisa.

"I'm weaving a crown of daisies into your hair."

"Then I'll look a fine mess when they wilt."

"If we can enjoy them for a quarter of an hour, sure that's enough," responded Dorcas, scrambling to her feet. "Ready?"

"Hey! Look – a cock fight!'" shouted Hefin, and they all rushed to follow him.

Dorcas stood on tiptoe, straining to see over the heads of the crowd that'd gathered in a tight circle around a small patch of bare earth. There was nothing like the sight of two cocks, going at each other's throats. The larger bird held himself upright, in complete control of proceedings, while the smaller one danced, ineffectively, about its opponent. Suddenly, the weakling lunged at the larger bird's neck and was harshly punished for his troubles. Feathers flew everywhere and it wasn't long before blood oozed from the defeated bird's neck. A moment later, it was stretched out in the mud, fading fast.

"A tuppence ha'penny fight, if ever I saw one. Two chickens would've fought better," commented one of the onlookers.

"Pity the poor punters who put money on the game," piped up someone else.

Lisa put her arm through Dorcas's and looped in Elsi with the other.

"I've had the most wonderful day," said Elsi, "and now ..."

"I can't wait for my supper!" exclaimed the other two, bursting into laughter.

"You rascals," said Elsi, but she couldn't help smiling. That's what friends were – the people who knew you better than anyone else.

At the ribbon stand, each girl bought a fine ribbon and a piece of lace to take home with them, agreeing that this was the best possible way to end a wonderful day.

* * *

Dorcas woke suddenly that night, and the first thing she heard was the sound of her little sister, Mabli, breathing next to her. Through the small window, she could see that it was a bright, moonlit night. She crept out of bed and went to gaze at the moon's radiance.

Ever since she was small, Dorcas had been fascinated by the moon. Somehow, that big ball of light could transform the everyday world and make of it a fairytale.

"Full be the moon, the owl does hoot, and robbers are a-coming in their knitted boots ..."

She longed to go outside. What secrets would reveal themselves in the darkness of night? If she saw the little people dancing in a circle, would she dare to join their dance, to follow them to the world beyond?

"What are you doing?" mumbled Mabli, somewhere between sleep and waking.

"Staring at the moon."

"Come back to bed."

"I can't sleep a wink. I fancy a walk in the moonlight."

"Dorcas ..."

All it took was for Mabli to plead with her like this, and Dorcas's heart would always melt. There were five years between them and Dorcas felt very protective of her little sister – yet, sometimes, you'd have been forgiven for wondering which of them was the eldest.

"You're all excited still after the dance, Dorcas. Come back here and give me a hug."

So Dorcas obeyed, returning to the warmth of their bed.

There was nothing more comforting than holding her sister in her arms. All her little worries disappeared.

"You better now?" Mabli asked her sister.

"I'm warmer."

"Who did you dance with? "

"Everyone ... but I got a smile from Rhys."

"He's nice," murmured Mabli, falling happily back to sleep.

But Dorcas couldn't sleep. The row she'd had from her father when she'd got home that night was still playing on her mind. When she'd stepped through the door there'd been a look on him like the very devil. Her mother had been busy about the hearth.

"Dorcas, you're finally home. Your father's not happy."

And Dorcas knew why at once.

"But you knew I was going down to the Marian ..." The Marian was the field, down by the river, where fairs were always held.

"On the feast day!" her father said.

"But ... everybody was there."

"And you danced, I expect."

"Yes."

"And what have we told you about that?"

Dorcas stared down at her shoes, the same shoes that had danced so sweetly just a short while earlier. She was that kind of girl – there was no point in denying it – a girl who liked to dance. Did that make her bad?

"Answer me."

"Your father's worried about you," said her mother quietly.

"As it was a holiday, I didn't see the harm in it. It was only a bit of fun."

Nobody said anything for a moment.

"Do you understand why dancing is bad, Dorcas? Why the Methodists consider it a sin?"

"Yes, Father," she replied, like a parrot, then she changed her mind. "Well, to be honest, no, I don't."

Her father sighed. This one was hard work, no doubt about it.

"Dancing itself is not a sin, but, rather, what it can lead to," he replied, as if he addressing a small child. "You're old enough to know what I'm talking about ..."

Dorcas had no choice but to lower her head in silence.

"When the festivities become unrestrained and out of control, that's when the Devil takes his place. He's a wily foe and he knows exactly how to play on our weaknesses and lusts."

Dorcas thought of the way Rhys had smiled at her. Hadn't that been the most natural thing in the world?

"I'm sorry, Father."

"We only have your best interests in mind, Dorcas. Good night."

"Good night," replied Dorcas, heading for the loft.

It was a bitter end to what had been such a wonderful day.

Chapter 2

Leaning her head against Neli's flank, Dorcas felt the heat of the sun on her nape. It was a lovely morning, and the birds were singing. As the milk pail slowly filled she enjoyed the comfort of the cow's warm body. It was good to have a few minutes' peace in the early morning, free of all the household bustle. It didn't last long, however, as Dorcas spotted Lewis approaching her, a crust of bread in one hand, an empty cup in the other. Lewis was five years old and always up to mischief.

"You finished yet?" he asked.

"Almost."

"Can I have a drop?"

Dorcas dipped his cup into the pail and handed it to her brother, watching as he gulped down the milk, drops dribbling down his face.

"Mam wants you to help with the washing ... can I help you take Neli back?"

"Of course you can."

Dorcas reached down for her little brother's hand, but he pulled away.

"I'm a big boy now."

"You'll have to take Neli yourself so," Dorcas teased, and the little lad thought for a moment.

"Better if Dorcas comes with Lewis."

"Good idea."

And they both returned to Cae Uchaf, or the High Field, with the cow, Dorcas watching Lewis's short legs jogging ahead and smiling at his attempt to appear older than he really was.

Back at the house, as she stepped through the door, Dorcas saw the clothes in a pile on the floor and her mother holding the baby. The water was boiling over the fire.

"Put the water in the tub. The baby's not so well today."

"Lewis is helping Dorcas today," announced Lewis.

"Best you don't, love," replied his mam. "Not with boiling water. Maybe Lewis can do something else ..."

"Like cutting wood?"

"We've got enough wood in already, Lewis," said Dorcas. "Come out with me here, and you can do your A B C."

As Dorcas scrubbed the clothes outside, Lewis was happy enough shaping letters in the soil with a stick.

"Can I learn a new letter?"

"How about you do 'L' for Lewis?" said Dorcas, taking the stick and drawing the letter.

"It's like a corner, isn't it?"

"It is. Remember 'Lewis' starts with the shape of a corner."

Lewis soon got bored with the letters and wanted something else to do.

"I'll tell you what would help, Lewis – why don't you collect tufts of sheep's wool from the hedges?"

"Lewis is not so well today," he replied.

"It's little Deio who's not so well. Lewis, on the other hand, is a big strong boy."

"Why have I got to collect wool?"

"Because we've none left and without it, I can't spin yarn, and if I don't spin yarn we can't weave ..."

"And if we can't weave, Lewis won't get any supper," he finished.

Her brother had heard this one plenty of times before, so off he went, grumbling loudly for Dorcas's benefit.

Washing day was always a long day at Tyddyn Pricia, the cottage where they lived. Boiling the water always took ages, but at least on a fine day the washing could all be done outdoors.

They scoured and scrubbed all morning, drawing and carrying more water, boiling it over the fire then rinsing the clothes in clean water before spreading them all out on the hedges to dry.

As Deio was sick, Dorcas had to do more than her share of the work today. Ifan, the eldest son, was working out in the fields with his father and, come evening, it was good to sit down to supper. By then, Deio was feeling better, much to his mother's relief.

"A fine meal," said Elis Edwards, scraping his plate clean then settling down by the fire to warm himself. "We must always be thankful for what God provides."

His wife, Ann, sat opposite him, carding wool.

"We must thank Mabli and Lewis today too," she said. "They've worked hard collecting wool from the hedges."

Mabli was ten years old, and she wasn't about to let the chance of scolding her brother pass by.

"Lewis got lost but I found him in the end."

"I wanted to go that way, that's why!" Lewis countered. "If you know where you're going, you're not lost, are you?"

"Tell the truth now. You've never been down that way before."

"Yes, well, I'm an adventurer," Lewis responded proudly and his parents looked at one another and smiled. That was Lewis in a nutshell.

Ifan lounged by the fire too, busy with his chisel, lost in an intricate design. At seventeen, he was two years older than Dorcas.

"What are you making there, Ifan?" asked Dorcas. "Carving a love spoon, are you?"

"No, I'm not."

"Yes, you are. Look, Mam, he's shaping a ball inside a square – isn't it good?"

"Let's see it, Ifan," said his mother, but Ifan was reluctant to show his handiwork.

"I'm just seeing if I can carve a ball, that's all."

"Well, it'll come in handy some day when you find a sweetheart," said Dorcas, teasing her brother.

Dorcas was at the spinning wheel, spinning yarn to give her mother a rest. The wool that Mabli and Lewis had collected was already washed and ready for working. Dorcas had been spinning since she was twelve years old, and Mabli sat at her side now, eager to learn.

"When you're spinning you're never still, Mabli. You have to keep a constant eye on the wheel. See? I'm feeding the wool through this end with my left hand, twisting it constantly. Forward, back, forward, back ..." Dorcas explained, swaying gently back and forth. "Your whole body moves, not just your arms. Half the secret is working together with the wheel."

"Can I try it?"

"It's high time for you and Lewis to be in bed," answered her mother. "Up you go now!"

"But Mam, Dorcas is in the middle of teaching me something!"

"Mabli dear, there's always tomorrow. Dorcas and I spin every day of the year, so I'm sure you'll get another chance."

"Tomorrow?"

"Yes, tomorrow – and the day after, and the day after that again." Her mother's voice was tired.

As she fell asleep that night, Mabli told herself her favourite story, the one about the girl who lived in the castle and spun straw into gold on a spinning wheel. Mabli insisted on calling her Sigl-di-gwt – or Wag-tail. She loved the name Sigl-di-gwt.

As soon as Dorcas came to bed, Mabli began:

"What was Sigl-di-gwt's castle like?"

"Oh, it was really magnificent, really grand, with high towers."

Dorcas stared up at the straw roof of their cottage, at the heather stuffed into the corners to keep the wind out.

"Would you like to live in a castle, Dorcas?"

"Only if its roof didn't leak and it wasn't cold or damp ..."

"Oh, don't worry! Our castle wouldn't be leaky or damp and we'd never be cold either. We'd always have a nice fire going in every room and servants and maids to look after us.

We'd have wonderful food to eat, on silver plates ..."

"Would we really?" said Dorcas, smiling in the darkness. "And would we have pudding too?"

"For sure. We'd have small delicate sweets with sugar like crystal on top, and fruit that no one would ever have seen the likes of before ..."

"You're making me hungry now ... stop, will you?"

"And after we've eaten, we'll dance until the wee small hours – me in my scarlet, wine-coloured dress that's covered in lace, and you – what kind of dress would you have?"

"It'd be blue, the colour of bluebells, and I'd have a host of ribbons in my hair," said Dorcas.

"Would you like a lace collar, too?"

"Of course. And what about lovely music?"

"There'd be a harp and violins playing ... it would be like being in heaven."

"But the night would have to end at some stage, Mabli."

"Only when we could dance no more. And then we'd retire to a huge bed with a soft, feather mattress and coverlet of red velvet with golden roses."

"Go to sleep, Mabli, and stop your rattling on," Dorcas laughed, snuggling down beneath the woollen blanket.

"But it would be nice all the same, wouldn't it?" Mabli murmured, sleepily.

Chapter 3

When Dorcas returned from feeding the chickens, she saw
Ifan's back as he worked the loom in the hut. Her father had
risen as dawn broke to work in the fulling mill, while Ifan's
task was to weave.

Dorcas watched from behind as Ifan drew the shuttle back
and forth.

"Deio's feeling better this morning, thank God. I hate it
when the poor little thing is ill," she said.

"I know. He's not himself when he's feeling sick," replied
Ifan. "Dad wasn't too good this morning either." This was
unusual.

Dorcas said, "Did you hear about the row I got for dancing?"

"Mam mentioned it."

"And you didn't get a telling-off?"

"No. Because I wasn't dancing!"

"But you were drinking with your friends and enjoying
yourself as much as I was."

"I'm older, and I'm a boy."

"It isn't as if I'm a flighty girl. There are loads of sillier
girls than me."

"But Mam and Dad aren't responsible for them, are they?"
Ifan raised his head and smiled. "They've given out to me
before – lots of times – much worse than you got. They're just
worried about you."

"It's enough to put me off going to Soar Chapel," retorted Dorcas.

"Watch out – you'll get an even worse telling off for that!"

Dorcas fell silent, watching her brother at his craft, impressed by his skill.

"You'll have to teach me to weave, Ifan. Mabli wanted me to teach her to spin yesterday – so maybe now's my chance."

"Keep the thread taut as you feed it through – that's the secret," said Ifan, deftly wielding the shuttle. "But you've enough on your plate already, preparing the wool and spinning it."

"But it's monotonous, like all housework," Dorcas replied. "At least you need skill to handle a loom."

"Maybe. But this gets monotonous enough after a while too."

Dorcas fingered the bundles of cloth.

"Depends how inventive you are, Ifan – how much you spice it up. If I had the chance, I'd put a purple stripe on each end – that'd finish things off nicely, wouldn't it?"

"They don't want purple stripes, Dorcas! They want a plain Welsh flannel, miles and miles of it, nothing fancy ..."

"It wouldn't cost us a penny extra. If we used moss dye, we could make green yarn, and purple is even easier. "

"It'd cost us more time. They don't pay us to go out gathering moss and doing fancy things like that."

"Who are 'they', anyway?" asked Dorcas.

"The traders in Shrewsbury. Keeping the price low with cheap materials – that's all they care about."

"And who buys such plain, miserable cloth?"

"Most of it's for soldiers and slaves," said Ifan, "so it's their owners that buy it. There must be masses of soldiers and slaves out there – seeing as they buy so much of it."

Soldiers and slaves, thought Dorcas. Such people were beyond her ken. But if Welsh cloth was what they wore, then this was a godsend for her family, for it kept the wolf from their door. As she stepped out of the hut, Dorcas paused and asked,

"Did you say that Dad wasn't well?"

"He was suffering with his back, poor creature. He doesn't look well, have you noticed? And he gets tired a lot quicker than he used to. I'm doing what I can to ease the load on him – but he's not getting any younger."

Her father, getting older? Dorcas hadn't thought of this before. She'd always imagined that her parents would stay the same forever, that only children changed. She didn't like to think of her parents growing old.

* * *

Next day, Dorcas and Ifan's job was to take the woollen cloth down to the fulling mill. Though it meant climbing up over the hill then making their way down to the river, it was a pleasant enough journey in fine weather, though their packs were heavy.

"We'll have a good appetite on us after this journey," said Dorcas, as they crested the hill and came down the other side.

"True," answered her brother. "But I'm not sure how often we'll be doing it again."

"Why not?" Dorcas couldn't imagine their day without the carding, the spinning and the weaving. It was so much part of their family life.

"They say the market's not what it was."

Dorcas hurried to keep up with Ifan, who was striding ahead.

"But that's really serious. If people don't want the cloth, what'll we do?"

"Don't worry when there's no cause to yet, Dorcas. Perhaps it's just a rumour."

They walked on silently towards the mill, deep in thought about a world that was changing fast. Things seemed so settled in Dolgellau that Dorcas had thought they'd stay like this forever. But in another two years she'd be the same age as Ifan, and Ifan would be of marriageable age and might well have left home. Mabli wouldn't be a little girl any more ...

Sometimes, her mother would sigh and say, "It's best we don't know what lies ahead for us," sending a shiver down Dorcas's spine. Dorcas was a hopeful person, someone who looked forward happily, in the belief that better days would come.

* * *

Sunday was always a big day at Tyddyn Pricia. The Sabbath chores were always completed the night before and, come morning, Ann Edwards made sure that each of her children dressed in their best clothes before setting off for Soar Chapel. In times gone by, everyone in the village had attended the church in the town but, in recent years, most people had turned their back on the Church and attended the chapels instead. Although Ann and her family went to chapel, Ann's sister had stayed true to the Church, mostly because her husband worked for a rich family who lived nearby.

Church language was English and Latin, while chapel services were held in Welsh. Dorcas often got bored with sermons, especially if they went on for too long, but she enjoyed learning to read and write in Sunday school.

"Teach me how to weave, will you?" Dorcas said to Ifan as they walked home from the chapel together.

"You're determined to master the craft, aren't you?"

"Well, if Dad or yourself were away from home, or if either of you were ill, it'd be awfully handy if I could handle the loom, wouldn't it?"

Ifan saw the determination in his sister's eyes and knew there was no point arguing. There was no point telling her that weaving was men's work either, or that women didn't usually do it. That was one things he loved about Dorcas – her invincible spirit, and her convinction that nothing was impossible for her.

The very next morning Ifan explained the different parts of the loom to Dorcas, who hung on his every word.

"These are the warp threads, and they're what keep the cloth taut. And this here's the shuttle."

"I know that much already, sure."

"Once you've wound the wool on to the shuttle, all you need do is feed it through, back and forth, on alternate threads ..." continued Ifan, demonstrating on the frame.

"These form the weft threads. To make sure the weft is kept tight, we need to keep an eye on the warp."

"It's like plaiting, isn't it? When I braid Mabli's hair, that's what I do – make sure that one strand's pulled tightly between two others."

"The principle's the same, except when you plait you weave several threads together at the same time," Ifan said, absorbed in his work. "Don't pull it too tight either, that's as bad as having it too loose."

"And that's all there is to it?"

"Yes, but of course you have to concentrate. But there's not a lot that can go wrong, if you keep the warp and weft threads in their place. It's all about practice."

"Can I try it?"

"I don't want this flannel ruined ..."

"How could I ruin it with you keeping your eagle eye on me?"

Ifan smiled and made room for her.

"Come here then," he said.

Of course, once Dorcas had started she refused to give up and so Ifan let carry on. She was learning fast, fair play.

"If ever you make your own flannel," said Ifan, "you must promise me one thing."

"What's that?"

"You have to resist the temptation to add different-coloured stripes to it."

Dorcas grinned. "I'll do just as you say, Master."

"You've never been under any master's thumb. And God help anyone who'd try to control you, Dorcas Edwards!"

Chapter 4

It was Mabli and Dorcas's turn to go down to town and sell eggs. Mabli had collected them early in the morning, and she'd found quite a haul.

"My favourite hen is Heti. She comes to say hello, while the others ignore me," said Mabli, entering the kitchen and noticing Lewis on his knees, giving milk to a suckling lamb. Dorcas went over to stroke it.

"Look at this little fellow, Dorcas. He takes the milk straight from my bottle."

"So he does. He likes you, I think."

"I can't come down to town with you today," Lewis said. "I'm too busy with important jobs here."

"That's a shame," said Mabli, putting the eggs into a basket. "Has the little lamb lost its mam?"

"No," replied Lewis. "His mami didn't want him and wouldn't let him suckle her. Poor little thing, and him being so sweet."

As Mabli went out the door with the eggs, Dorcas heard Lewis say, quietly, "Wouldn't it be an awful thing if Mami didn't want me, just like this lamb's mami?"

"Lewis, don't say such a thing! Mam thinks the world of you."

"Yes, but she gets cross with me sometimes." There was no milk left in the bottle now.

"Only when you play up. But you mean the whole wide world to us all, you know that." Dorcas felt for her brother.

"I like it when you tell me things like that," said the little boy, and Dorcas felt warm inside. She loved his innocence.

Just then, their mother hurried in. "Get a move on now, girls, or the market will be over before you get there!"

On their way to town, Mabli chattered ten to a dozen. Her favourite game was playing at 'rich people'.

"Let's pretend we're wearing costly silk dresses and the finest of pearls around our necks."

Dorcas looked at her sister's outfit, which was ragged and too small for her. You needed quite an imagination to turn it into a silk dress.

"Mabli, if we were rich, we wouldn't have to sell eggs."

"No, and we wouldn't be walking, either. We'd travel in a fine coach instead with all the people looking at us as we passed by. But I'd throw pennies to the poor."

"No you wouldn't. If you were rich, you wouldn't care about the poor."

* * *

Dolgellau's square was full of bustle as people arrived at market, the stallholders having risen before cock-crow to arrange their goods. Vegetables, meat, herbs, oats, honey, lace, ribbons, flowers, cloth and leather goods – it was a feast of scents and colours. Whatever you wanted, you'd have found it at Dolgellau Market that day – for a price. Many had come from afar, and they wove through each other within the crowd while children ran excitedly amongst them, chasing after a dog, a ball or a hoop, shouting and laughing. Yes, there was fun to be had at the market.

Dorcas arranged her egg basket near Martha Gelli's cheese stall.

"How are you two this morning?" asked Martha cheerfully. "You hear that Elin Rhyd y Bedol had a baby last night? Great lump of a boy, at seven pounds."

"Does he have a name yet?"

"Guto Wyn, after his grandfather on his mother's side – the family from Sarnau."

"She's got one already, hasn't she?"

"Yes, Cadi – who's nearly two now. She's a little darling. Hopefully, I'll get to see them one of these days. I'll buy two eggs from you there …"

"Thank you, Martha."

"May I have half a dozen eggs, please?" asked a tall woman, who was standing behind Martha.

"That'll be thruppence ha'penny, please," said Mabli. She was in her element serving customers.

Dorcas turned to her. "Mabli, are you all right on your own for a while? Elsi's over there at the vegetable stall."

Mabli nodded, turning to serve another customer, while Dorcas hurried towards her friend.

"Dorcas, how are you?" said Elsi. "It's amazingly busy here. You coming over to the Society tomorrow night?"

"Yes, I'm looking forward to it. Dad hasn't been well and we've a lot of work on, but I'd say Mam can do without me for an hour or two."

Elsi smiled. "Rhys Fychan will be there," she said with a wink.

"And who've you got your eye on?"

Elsi blushed. "His friend's nice, but he won't look at me if Gwenno's there."

And the two girls chatted until Elsi's mother told her to pay attention to the customers.

When Dorcas returned to her stand, Mabli's face was as cross as a bear.

"Where have you been for so long? I've sold over half the eggs since you left!"

"Never you mind."

"You haven't got a sweetheart, have you, Dorcas? Hey, Dorcas – have you?" Mabli went on, sensing secrets.

"Never you mind. I wouldn't tell you now anyway, even if I had."

Mabli sulked. At this moment she hated Dorcas for being so much older than her.

"It's my turn to wander about now," said Mabli after a bit.

"Where are you going?"

"I'd like to see the ribbon and lace stand – it's only over there."

"All right, but don't dawdle."

"Well you're a fine one to talk, aren't you?" mumbled Mabli under her breath.

Dorcas soon sold the rest of the eggs, then she noticed a man placing a wooden box on the ground and standing on it. He began to speak, but she couldn't hear him properly, so she left the stand and moved closer. Soon a small crowd had gathered in a circle around him – unexpected entertainment like this was always worth a look.

The speaker was a man of about thirty with auburn hair and an intense look on his face.

"So what do you say to what I've just told you?" asked the man. "Will you turn a deaf ear and walk away? Or will you speak out against slavery?" He stared intently into the crowd. "The people I speak of are men and women just like you and me – with hearts that beat, and bodies that bleed red, the same as ours. They feel the same things that we do. And their bodies will perish and rise from the tomb the same as will ours. Their souls will live in the world to come – just as will ours. The only difference between us is the colour of our skin, and this is no reason to treat them like animals."

You could have heard a pin drop; he held the crowd in the palm of his hand.

"They denounce the slaves for rising up and rebelling against their masters, yet what choice do they have?"

Dorcas had never heard anyone speak with so much passion.

"Even if you gave them the best food and wine, they are still slaves. If they are dressed in silks and lace, they are still slaves. If they live in castles and sleep on feather beds, they are still slaves. Because they have nothing, they own nothing – not the clothes on their back, not their own bodies, not even their children.

"From dawn to dusk, they toil in the fields beneath the raging heat of the sun – sweating in rags, whipped mercilessly. They are treated like animals and killed for the slightest of excuses. I heard of a slave-girl feeding her baby at her breast – the most natural thing in the world – and her punishment was the lash.

"Brothers and sisters, the sound of their cries, the flood of their tears, their suffering sighs ... they reach us here in Wales from the Caribbean. We cannot allow this trade in people to continue."

The man next to her turned to Dorcas.

"What's he rambling on about?"

"Slaves," said Dorcas. "About how we treat black people."

"Who's black round here?" the man asked, looking about him. "I don't see any. Why's he going on about black people in Dolgellau?"

"I couldn't afford a servant nor a slave," said another man. "What is he, a missionary?"

"I don't know what the devil he is," said a third man, who smelled of drink, "but Dolgellau's no place for him."

"He's lost his way to Mallwyd, if you ask me."

"He surely has. Black men's rights, by hell. What about the rights of us Welsh?" and the rest shouted their applause.

From somewhere, an egg came hurtling at the speaker, and then things got messy. Dorcas hoped it wasn't one of their eggs. Martha Gelli approached with her arm round Mabli's shoulders, and her young sister's face was stained with tears.

"Here we are, we've found Dorcas at last! The poor thing thought she'd lost you."

Dorcas felt terribly ashamed that she'd been so absorbed in the man's speech that she'd forgotten her sister.

"I'm sorry, Martha. Thanks for looking after her."

"No need to thank me, honestly." Martha was looking about her at the dispersing crowd.

"Which one's your sweetheart then?" she asked with a wink, before turning back to town.

As they too made their way home up Allt Ganol, Mabli asked, "What was the man on the box talking about?"

"Did you hear him?"

"It was hard not to. He was louder than any preacher I've ever heard," she said, swinging the basket to and fro. "The people who are whipped and cry and get treated like animals – who are they?"

"Slaves."

"What are they?" asked Mabli, full of curiosity.

"Black people who have to work terribly hard."

"Poor them. But where are they?"

"They live a long way away, over the sea in the Caribbean."

"But why are people so cruel to them?"

"Because they're black, I expect." The man's speech had shaken Dorcas, making her think. And now here was Mabli with her endless questions.

"But they didn't choose to be black, did they?"

"No, no more than we chose to be white."

Mabli was quiet for a while, and Dorcas paused so her sister could catch her up.

"I don't understand," said the little girl. "Why did he come to Dolgellau to say that – about the black people, the – what were they called again?"

"They're called slaves, Mabli."

"Yes, those. What have we got to do with them?"

"It's us that make their clothes."

Mabli stopped in her tracks, staring at Dorcas in astonishment.

"Who?"

"Us – we make the cloth. You know the flannel that we weave and gets sold and goes to Shrewsbury? Well, that's the cloth that goes to the Caribbean, and it's used to make clothes for the slaves."

Mabli began walking again and her worried expression disappeared.

"Well, that's a kind thing to do for the slaves, isn't it? If it wasn't for the people of Dolgellau, they'd be naked."

"True," replied Dorcas. But, clothes or not, it was still terrible to think that some people were cruelly whipped and that other people treated them so appallingly.

Chapter 5

While Dorcas and Mabli were at the market, their mother was busy baking and Lewis was supposed to be keeping an eye on Deio.

"I want Dorcas," Lewis whined. "She was going to show me more letters." Minding a baby was no fun at all.

"They'll be back any minute now," said Ann Edwards as she placed the bread in the oven, before fetching the money tin. She emptied the pennies out onto the table.

"Hold on to Deio for a minute while I count this," she said.

"Can I help you with the sums, Mam?"

"Lewis, Mami wants a minute's peace … These pennies disappear faster every week."

Lewis watched his mother count them out. He was interested in things that disappeared.

Then he looked up at his mam. There was a worried look on her face, as there always was when she handled money.

Deio's little hand grabbed a penny and in no time he'd put it into his mouth.

"Lewis – take that out of his mouth! They're scarce enough as it is," scolded his mother.

"He's hungry," says Lewis, "he wants some food."

They always want food, thought Ann, her face creased with worry. More and more food, with less and less to pay for it.

"Money's a funny thing, isn't it?" piped up Lewis. "You can't eat it, but you can change it for things to eat."

"Money's a very funny thing all right," replied his mother, "and funnier still is that there's never enough of it to go around."

Just then, the door opened and Dorcas and Mabli came in. Lewis's face lit up and he lifted Deio to put him into in his big sister's arms.

"Here's a little bit more for the money tin," said Mabli, handing the money to her mam. "We sold them pretty quickly. I sold most of them ..." she went on, giving Dorcas a look.

"Well done you. I've put the bread in the oven, Dorcas," said Ann.

"Can I have a minute to catch my breath?" asked Dorcas.

"Lunch needs making now ... I'm almost finished with these."

Dorcas looked at the table and saw an envelope.

"You got a letter!" she said.

Ann snatched it away and pushed it under her apron.

"Bad news?" Dorcas asked, anxiously.

Her mother's eyes looked into hers.

"No, Dorcas, but I have something to tell you ... Listen, what about a cup of tea?" she said. Then she shouted for Mabli to look after the little ones – anywhere but the kitchen.

As Dorcas sat down, all sorts of things raced through her mind. Was her mother ill? Was someone else ill? Was something momentous about to be revealed to her? Her mam couldn't sit still – she was fiddling with the kettle, opening then closing the oven door, hurrying to fetch the teapot and cups. Dorcas had never seen her like this before.

"Mam ..."

"I'll be there now."

"It's about that letter, isn't it? Don't bother with the tea, just tell me."

But Ann Edwards had to do things her own way. At long last, she came to the table with the teapot and two cups.

"I wasn't going to do anything behind your back, but there was no point worrying you for no reason ..."

She sat down and looked at Dorcas, and then at the small piles of coins on the table. "You know things have been a bit tight recently ..."

"No worse than usual ..." Then, catching her mother's anxious expression, "Or are they?"

Her mother stared down at the pennies.

"I don't want to worry you, children, but between everything – less work, your father not being well, prices rising ... Whatever, I sent word ... well, before that, I thought maybe you could go out to work ... as a maid."

Dorcas felt her stomach turn. One or two of her friends were maids, but she'd never considered such work herself.

"But there's more than enough work for me here."

Her mother reached for the letter.

"Yes, I know. That's what makes things difficult. I wrote to my sister, asking her if any work was to be had in Arfon, and if she'd said no such luck, then that would've been the end of it."

Dorcas looked at the letter then back at her mother.

"But ..."

"But Geini says there's work to be had – in Bangor."

Dorcas froze. If someone had thrown a bucket of cold water over her, she couldn't have had more of a shock.

"Bangor? But that's so far away!"

"You'll need to think it over first, but it's very good work, in a grand mansion. You'll get your bed and board and earn a wage and we'd have one less mouth to feed here. Your cousin Cadi's working as a maid there already and they'll be sure to treat you well, Dorcas ..."

Then Lewis came racing into the room, with Deio and Mabli close on his heels.

"I smell burning, Mam," said Mabli.

"The bread!" shouted her mother, hurrying to pull two loaves out of the oven.

Mabli came to the table with Deio in her arms, and Lewis couldn't take his eyes off the hot bread. Dorcas watched them, as if from afar. This was her family and this was where she belonged – she couldn't imagine herself anywhere else. Her life was about to shatter into pieces.

The kitchen filled with the smell of fresh bread.

"They're not too bad," said her mother with a sigh of relief. "It could've been a lot worse."

But Dorcas couldn't see how things could be any worse. She got to her feet and made for the back door like someone in a trance.

"Dorcas, don't go now!" shouted her mam.

"I just want some fresh air."

"Yes, but we have to make lunch for this lot, and I'm busy with the dough ..."

Dorcas turned back to make bread and milk for everyone as questions crowded into her mind.

"How long would I have to stay in this place, Mam?"

Her mother sighed. "I don't know, Dorcas. Nothing's been decided yet. What about having a bite to eat first ? Mabli, go and call Ifan, will you?"

Chapter 6

As she worked at the loom, Dorcas stared at the woven material with its straight, consistent lines, like the pattern of her future. There was no doubt about it now – she'd have to go to Bangor. She'd turned the matter over and over in her mind, and there was no way out. She'd even asked her friends, those who were already in service, whether there was any work going around here. Being a maid locally would be a thousand times better than going as far as Bangor.

She led the shuttle through the weft, put her foot on the treadle to lift the warp, moved the batten down onto the weft, then repeated the task. For some weeks now she'd mastered the art of weaving. She'd believed that this would be her future – helping her mother at home, looking after the children, washing and cooking, spinning and weaving. She didn't want any more from life.

Yes, life could be monotonous, but wasn't everyone's life boring sometimes? She'd never imagined that this could happen to her – that she'd be torn away from everything familiar to her – home, family, friends, chapel – only to be sent to a unknown, faraway place.

"It won't be completely unknown. Cadi will be there," her mother had tried to tell her a hundred times. But though her cousin was close enough to her in age, Dorcas didn't know her at all. Lisa, Elsi and Sara were her friends, friends she'd known since she was a little child. She'd have to break her connection with them. And even if she did come home after a year, things wouldn't be the same. Their lives would have moved on without her. And Rhys, Rhys Fychan, who was so dear to her – he'd find another girl to smile at and to win her heart.

Dorcas would be a maid. Just a maid. She didn't even know what a maid did. A skill like weaving would be of no use in a mansion. She'd be cleaning, sweeping and scrubbing floors from morning till night. Life would be horrible ... Dorcas stopped to look at her work, and felt the tears welling in her eyes. Then she heard a sound outside and her father came in.

"Your mother's broken the news to you, then," he said gently.

Dorcas nodded, letting the tears fall. Her father came to her and held her tightly.

"I'm sorry. We'd give the world to keep you here with us."

Dorcas leaned against him and held her father close. If her father couldn't help her, then it was over for her.

"It's so far away, Dad."

Elis Edwards gave a sigh.

"I know. You'll need strong armour to face what lies ahead."

Dorcas looked at him.

"What does that mean?"

"This is what the Word teaches us. 'For our light affliction, which is but for a moment, worketh for us a far more exceeding and eternal weight of glory.' We need only place our hope in Jesus Christ, and he'll take care of us."

"So I'm supposed to accept the situation."

"We're not pretending it'll be easy. It's not easy for me to accept that my health is fading, or that the woollen trade is in decline. But we must accept the burdens that life throws at us. 'For I have learned, in whatsoever state I am, therewith to be content', as Paul tells us."

Dorcas wished her father wouldn't spout verses from the Scriptures. Such words might help him, but they didn't lift her heart. She wanted the comfort of her father's words, not the Apostle Paul's.

So Dorcas didn't have the chance to take or refuse the offer of working as a maid. Everyone accepted that it would happen, and they swept her along with them. When the youngest members of the family were told, Mabli was jealous.

"So you don't want to go?"

Dorcas was spinning wool and Mabli was carding.

"No. Not at all." Dorcas stared at the wheel as it spun.

"Mam says you're going to a grand house – more than grand. She said it was a castle."

"It's called Penrhyn Castle. I'm not sure it's a real Castle, but there's a lord there called Lord Penrhyn."

Mabli's eyes were like saucers.

"You know what this means – all of our dreams are coming true! How many times have we dreamed of living in a grand mansion?"

"I'll be going there to work as a maid, Mabli."

Their mother had made a cake, and Mabli was holding the bowl, licking the remains that clung to its sides.

"So what? The son of the mansion will be amazed at your

beauty and will want to marry you. Then you won't have to work at all. You'll wear a beautiful dress, the colour of bluebells, and you'll be a lady."

For once, Dorcas had no patience with her sister's foolish dreams.

"It's time you began to realise how things are in in the real world. Grow up, will you," she said bitterly.

Mabli glanced quickly at her sister, obviously cut to the quick.

"Things like that can happen! I've heard enough stories about poor girls melting the hearts of rich men. It's not impossible, and you have a much better chance if you're working in a castle! Don't be so sad-mannered, Dorcas."

Dorcas stared at what was before her – at the flour and sugar on her sister's cheeks, the dishes covering the table, the messiness of everyday life that filled the place.

"I don't want to leave here but no one's listening to me," she said bitterly.

Mabli got up.

"All right! If you don't want to go, maybe Mam and Dad will let me go instead ..."

"Don't be stupid. You're too young, sure."

Mabli stood before her, full of defiance.

"I'll be eleven next birthday, and girls that age can be maids." She grabbed Dorcas's arm. "Oh Dorcas, we'll never get a chance like this again! Let's both of us go there to work. We'd be company for each other, and everything would work out fine."

Dorcas imagined her sister, joining her, and how wonderful that would be.

"That'd be lovely, Mabli. Maybe you'll be able to come in a year or two …"

"You won't forget about me?"

Dorcas reached out to wrap her arm around her little sister.

"I'll miss you more than anyone – you and your crazy dreams."

"A year's a long time." Mabli looked up at her sister. "You'll have new clothes, won't you … what will they be like?"

"They won't be much better than the flannel we weave. They'll be work clothes for scrubbing on my knees and blacking hearths …"

Mabli whispered in Dorcas's ear. "It's only for a little while, remember … then I'll arrive, and you'll see how dreams can come true. One thing you can be sure of – it'll be completely different from Dolgellau!"

That was Dorcas's greatest fear.

"You know what I'll do, Mabli? I'll send you a letter describing the place and the work and all the grand ladies. Would you like that?"

Mabli's face was a picture.

"No one's ever written me a letter. Oh, thank you, Dorcas."

And Mabli hugged her sister, gripping her tightly in an embrace that expressed so much love that Dorcas knew she would never forget it.

Chapter 7

Dorcas lurched back and forth, back and forth, and as her body jolted her thoughts were pulled here and there too. She was on a cart, and its squeaking wheels were all she could hear. Every now and then she'd be winded as the cart struck a pothole and pitched wildly. If only the jolting would stop for a bit, Dorcas could try to organise her thoughts.

She'd set off on her way almost before she'd realised it. How had things happened so quickly? Should she have put up more of a fight? But what would've been the point? The decision had already been made ... Dorcas was leaving home and going to work as a maid at the other end of the world. She might as well have been on her way to Australia.

The arrangements had all been one big rush in the end. When they'd got wind that Robin Gyrrwr, the cart driver, was going three-quarters of the way to Bangor with his cart and was leaving in five days' time, it had been too good an offer to pass up. There'd been no order to the farewells, or to the packing. Dorcas had flung her things together, higgledy piggledy, and snatched a short hour with Lisa and Elsi, who couldn't believe she was really going. Neither could Dorcas, in those last few days at Tyddyn Pricia, as she watched Deio, sleeping in his cradle, or explained to Lewis and Mabli where she was going. Everyone told her she'd be back, but no one knew when. And if she did return, she wouldn't be the same Dorcas – that much was certain.

She remembered glancing over her shoulder for one last look at the town. She'd rarely travelled beyond Dolgellau in her life. These formed the borders of her world. Now, with no one to keep her company, she'd been thrown out with no one to depend on but herself. She was too young to have to do this. She was quiet throughout the journey, and the driver soon realised that she wasn't in the mood for chat. Tyddyn Pricia's eldest girl was usually a cheerful enough lass, he reflected, but she was sulking today. She was obviously leaving home against her will.

But it was fear of what lay ahead that Dorcas felt – and this was a new feeling. Until now, she'd looked forward to growing up, and all the excitement that was to come. It's true she'd often complained that life wasn't exciting enough, but the really important thing was having the company of family and friends. Now, as she was embarking on the greatest adventure of her life, she was paralysed by fear and loneliness. That didn't bode well.

Onwards went the horse and cart, and all Dorcas wanted to do was to turn back. Maybe Robin Gyrrwr had forgotten something, maybe he didn't feel well, maybe the horse would lose a shoe. But by the time they'd reach Ganllwyd, it was too late to hope for such things; every step the horse made took her further and further from Tyddyn Pricia and all that was familiar. Once she'd lost sight of Cader Idris, she knew she was in No Man's Land.

Her greatest regret was that she hadn't had the chance to

see Rhys. But even if she had, what would she have said to him? How was she meant to say goodbye, anyway … especially to someone she'd loved from afar? Even with her friends and family she hadn't known how to say goodbye properly – hadn't known what to do. One minute she was with her family, part of them, and the next they'd disappeared, like characters in a myth, and she was on this rickety cart, heading for oblivion … It was enough to send a person out of their mind.

She held the image of each member of her family in her memory – Mabli bursting with envy; Ifan sympathetic – the only one who really understood how she felt; Lewis knowing that something was wrong and sobbing his eyes out, and Deio, staring at her in bewilderment.

Dorcas had felt her own tears welling. She hadn't realised the true significance of the separation until her parents had held her so tightly that she could hardly breathe. It dawned on her then that something huge, a momentous turning point, was taking place in her life. Something from which she could never return.

When Betws-y-coed came into view, Robin Gyrrwr told Dorcas that he'd brought her as far as he could. He'd told her which road to take, and there was nothing for it then but to walk the last twenty miles to Penrhyn Castle.

"I hope things are better for you there than you fear – though I doubt very much that they will be." These were Robin Gyrrwr's parting words. Why had he said this? Was it a warning? What on earth was he expecting her to do? She thanked him politely and watched him on his way, until he and his cart were no more than a spot on the horizon.

Dorcas picked up her pack and set off in the direction of Dyffryn Ogwen. She felt as if she was walking towards the gallows.

* * *

How many times did Dorcas relive that journey in her mind, the long miles of walking through the valley of Dyffryn Ogwen to Llandegái and onto Penrhyn Castle? It was the exhaustion of it that stayed with her. In comparison, the journey on the cart with Robin Gyrrwr had been a pleasure trip. Mercifully, the day had stayed dry, she met no one else on the road so that her pack was her only travelling companion. As the day wore on, the sky darkened blood-red and Dorcas sat at the side of the road to reach for the packet her mother had prepared for her. In it was a piece of bread and cheese and she ate it eagerly – she was starving hungry by now – though she knew it would be her last bite for some time. How much further was there to go? In the distance loomed the mountain of mynydd Tryfan, staring menacingly down at her like an angry giant. All she saw about her were mountains. In this solitude there was not a house to be seen anywhere, let alone a castle.

An hour later, she had reached the end of her tether. She collapsed and sunk to her knees at the side of the hedge. If she didn't see anything soon she'd have no choice but to sleep in the hedge and start again in the morning. Then she saw a man, driving two cows, heading towards her.

"You look tired, my girl," he said. "Where are you headed?"

"Llandygái," answered Dorcas. "Is it far from here?"

"About two miles further on and you'll be there. Who do you know in Llandygái? If they're farming people, there's a good chance I'll know them."

"I'm going to Penrhyn Castle."

Was it Dorcas's imagination or had a dark shadow fallen across the man's eyes?

"Oh," he said, disappointed. "No, I don't know a living soul in that place."

He wished Dorcas well, and she continued her journey.

If Dorcas had known then what she knew later, she'd have turned on her heel and followed that man and his two cows all the way home. But that evening she still had faith in human nature. She thought she'd find a welcome at the end of her journey – food, warmth and a cosy bed to sleep in. She was so sure of this that the idea kept her going on the last part of her journey.

Then it started to rain.

Chapter 8

When Dorcas arrived at the gates of Penrhyn Castle it was approaching midnight. Her first thought was that the castle entrance looked like the Gates of Heaven, it was so grand and imposing. So it really was a castle, after all! The gateway was huge, with two towers flanking either side of a semi-circular archway. Above the entrance was an image carved into the stone. A shiver coursed down Dorcas's spine as she saw what it was – a warrior's arm about to bring an axe down onto a dragon. She had never seen a less welcoming image. Taking a stick, she struck the huge wooden door three times. No one answered. For a moment, Dorcas was afraid she'd come to the wrong place, but that was impossible. This was the largest building she'd seen on her journey, and it was definitely a castle. So she circled the building and found the back entrance, the door for the servants and maids.

She could tell that there were people inside from the shadows that moved in the dim light from one of the windows. She shouted again and again and hammered on the door with all the strength that remained in her exhausted body. Perhaps it was at this moment that she felt the most lonely. Suddenly she noticed a rope hanging at the side of the door and pulled it. She heard the sound of a bell and then, from the depths of the castle, came the sound of footsteps, approaching. The door opened. If Dorcas had been expecting a welcome, she was badly mistaken when, the next moment, a sour-faced man was glaring at her.

"Yes. And who are you?" said the bearded man in English, raising a lantern to peer at her face.

"Hello, I'm Dorcas," she replied in Welsh.

"Speak up, girl! What do you want?"

"I'm Dorcas, from Dolgellau ... I've come here to be a maid ... I'm a maid."

"Speak English! I can't understand a word you're saying."

"Dorcas Edwards – new work – here," Dorcas stuttered, dredging up the few English words that she knew.

"Don't know what you're on about. Come in, girl – we'll put you up till the mornin' and then you can explain to someone. Well? What are you waiting for? Come in!"

Dorcas stepped over the threshold and followed the tall man with the lantern down a long corridor. Then he pointed at a small room full of shoes and hats.

"Sleep there, and you can sort ye'self out in the mornin'. I'll find you a blanket. What you're doing landing in the middle o' the night, I've no idea," he said abruptly, leaving Dorcas on her own. He came back a moment later and threw a blanket at her.

Dorcas closed the door and looked about her, but there was no sign of a bed in the room. All she could see was a table with dirty shoes and silk hats on it, and a mess of brushes and cleaning gear. There was a chair by the fireplace and Dorcas sat there, laying the blanket over her. It was one of the most uncomfortable nights Dorcas had ever spent in her life, but exhaustion got the better of her and she fell asleep almost immediately. She could only imagine what poor Mabli would have said if she'd seen her here in such circumstances. She had a strange dream that night that the silk hats came to life and began to fly around the room and the dirty shoes began to kick, even though there were no feet in them.

She was awoken by the angry man, shaking her by the shoulders and telling her to get up. He ordered her to her feet, and after following him down more than one corridor and up more than one set of stairs she found herself in front of a pale-faced woman.

"Dorcas Edwards, I presume?"

"Yes!" Finally someone knew who she was.

"You took your time getting here. We were expecting you yesterday afternoon. You're a day late, girl!"

Dorcas's command of English wasn't that good and she decided that staying quiet was the best thing. She looked around at the cosy fireplace with a grand clock on its mantelpiece and knick-nacks in every corner of the room. So this was how the rich lived!

"Do you wish to apologise, or give us an explanation – presuming they haven't sent us a mute?"

The woman looked at her up and down, assessing her from head to foot.

"I know someone who's already working here – a maid called Cadi. Cadi Williams." Dorcas hoped her answer – in Welsh – would be enough.

"Kadi is your cousin, I understand."

In the end, after much confusion, Cadi was sent for to try and understand what was going on.

A few moments later the door opened and a thin, frail-looking girl with straight brown hair and expressionless eyes came in. She smiled the first smile Dorcas had seen in a long time. Dorcas looked for any family similiarities in her, but apart from the shape of her nose, there was nothing familiar about her. It was strange to think that the mothers of both girls were sisters.

"You didn't tell us that your cousin was a monoglot, Kadi."

Cadi didn't know what a 'monoglot' was and so she didn't respond.

The woman sighed, while Dorcas admired the lamp on the table and the cushions on the big armchair. Everything looked so clean and polished.

"A fine pair we have here. Let's hope her English will improve. In the meantime, you'll have to interpret for her. Do you understand, Kadi?"

Cadi had no idea what the word "interpret" meant either but she nodded.

"And what are you called again?"

"Dorcas, ma'am."

"What kind of a name is that? It's unpronouncable. I'll call her Edwards. She'd better be a good cleaner. Show her to her room and give her her uniform. She can stay with you until she learns the ropes. You may leave."

"Thanks, ma'am."

Cadi turned to Dorcas and spoke in Welsh. "We can go now. Follow me."

Dorcas followed her cousin through doorways and corridors like a rabbit warren. This castle was truly enormous. It was lucky that Cadi was with her, or she would have got completely lost, thought Dorcas as they reached Cadi's small attic bedroom.

Cadi turned to Dorcas and said,

"So welcome to Penrhyn Castle, Dorcas."

"I haven't started on the right foot with Lady Penrhyn, have I?"

"Who?"

"The cross lady we were just talking to ..."

"That wasn't Lady Penrhyn. That was Miss Grantham, the housekeeper!"

Dorcas felt foolish. Cadi stared her up and down, as if trying to work her out.

"But her room was so grand. I thought that ..."

"You've a lot to learn, haven't you?" said Cadi. "Miss Grantham can't pronounce 'Dorcas' so she's going to call you Edwards!"

They smiled at one another shyly.

"Come on, here are your clothes. Change quickly so we can go down to breakfast."

Dorcas looked at the small room, the pair of beds with the table between them, and the two chairs. 'Bare' was the only word to describe it. On the chair was a baggy grey dress and a calico cap. Dorcas put them on, and felt like a stranger. There was no shape to the dress at all, and the material felt rough on her skin. She put on the cap, hoping that it didn't look as odd as it felt.

On their arrival in the kitchen, almost thirty faces turned to look at the new maid.

Dorcas saw two long tables with benches on either side. On the walls were wooden panels, and the doors and windows were arched with half-circles. Dorcas followed her cousin to collect a bowl of porridge and was shown to her place at the end of a long bench. At the top of the table stood Miss Grantham. Dorcas took up her spoon, hungry for something to eat, but the girl next to her gave her a kick beneath the table.

"Hold your horses, what's wrong with you?"

Miss Grantham glared at Dorcas, with eyes the devil would've been pleased to call his own.

"Stand, Edwards."

"Stand up, Dorcas!" whispered Cadi from the other side of the table.

Blushing to the tips of her ears, Dorcas got to her feet, hating being the centre of attention.

"Good morning," began Miss Grantham. "As you see, we have a new member of staff – she's finally here. She's known as Edwards and she's one of the scullery maids. She presently speaks no English, so patience will be required with her. You may commence eating after saying Grace. Bless, O Father ... "

Then everyone raised their spoons to their mouths and began eating at exactly the same moment. No one said a word to each other, and Dorcas began to wonder what kind of a place this was. She already felt like a fish out of water but, even worse, she appeared equally strange to them. It was just as if she'd been thrown into a lunatic asylum.

Chapter 9

In her bare box-room months later, Dorcas remembered the image of the lunatic asylum that had come to her that morning. She'd known from that moment that she didn't fit into Penrhyn Castle's alien society, no matter how hard she tried. She should have made a run for it straight away, and left them to their gruel. Her father's verses came into her mind: 'For I have learned, in whatsoever state I am, therewith to be content.' But in her heart, she knew that the regime she had to abide by now was horribly wrong. What she didn't know yet was just how much worse it would become.

After breakfast on that first morning, everyone formed a line in the corridor in pairs, as if heading for Noah's ark.

Luckily, Cadi was by her side.

"What's going on?" Dorcas whispered to her.

"We're going to church."

"Church? I can't go to church. Father would kill me."

"Be quiet."

She saw faces turning to her in contempt.

Dorcas had to have her say. "But I'm a Methodist ..." she hissed beneath her breath.

"Quiet!" said Miss Grantham harshly. "Anyone caught talking will be punished."

Cadi closed her eyes and lowered her head. She was obviously anxious.

Dorcas wondered what she should do. The long line of servants moved up the stairs from the kitchen. Should she explain to Miss Grantham was she didn't attend church? She was afraid to do so. Then she thought how angry her father would be if he found out that she'd gone to church. But she walked on with the others, through corridors, under several arches, to a spectacular part of the building, then through the double doors of a church within the castle. She felt that she was being driven by a force outside of herself. Suddenly, she was aware of the splendour of the building, and its authority. She would never be able to walk out. She had to do what everyone else did. The servants and maids sat in their place and the service began.

The service was all in English, so Dorcas didn't understand a word. The only thing she could pick out was 'Our Lord', 'the Great Lord', Lord this and Lord the other – but the only lord she knew of was Lord Penrhyn. They didn't sing hymns as they did in chapel at home, they just chanted, and it sounded strange and soulless to Dorcas's ears. The singing of Pantycelyn's hymns was Dorcas's greatest pleasure at Soar Chapel and being denied them now was breaking her heart. She couldn't even recite the Lord's Prayer in English, so she whispered the words in Welsh to herself. Dorcas had never experienced so little blessing at a service. What's more, one of the man-servants stared at her throughout the service, making her feel even more uncomfortable.

The grand building was nothing like the chapel at home. In fact, she had never seen such an ornate place in her life. It wasn't that big, and the arched, white ceiling made Dorcas feel as if she was inside a giant shell. But the decorations! How in the world had they carved such beautiful designs and shapes? There was a cluster of six columns on either side, which came together from the ceiling. Every single column was carved in a different pattern. The priest's murmuring droned on while Dorcas explored the architecture with her eyes. Eventually, the priest closed the Bible, bowed before the altar, and the service ended. Dorcas gave a sigh of relief.

In silence, everyone marched from the church and through the door to the servants' quarters. Everyone else knew exactly where they were going, and Dorcas followed Cadi like a puppy.

"That was horrible," said Dorcas, the minute the two were on their own.

"You'll have to learn to shut your mouth, Dorcas – you can't talk when you want – it's a golden rule."

"But … it was completely against my nature to go to a church service!"

Cadi didn't even look at her.

"Learn to do things completely against your nature then," she told her, as if this was the easiest thing in the world. She opened a cupboard at the end of the corridor and took out cleaning equipment.

"Our first task is to clean the fireplaces. I've done some of the work before breakfast, but there's plenty still to do. Best you watch me and see how I do it first, and then you can try it for yourself."

"I'll never find my way around this place, it's so huge."

"You will. Everyone gets lost in the first few days."

Cadi took brushes from a box and handed Dorcas two buckets.

But Dorcas was still trying to get over the trauma of the church service.

"It feels so very uncomfortable being here," she said.

"A lot feels uncomfortable here. You'll get used to it."

"But I don't want to get used to it, Cadi!"

What's wrong with her? Dorcas thought. She seemed as calm as a mill-pond, as if nothing ever troubled her. Cadi sighed and walked ahead.

"Being a maid is one thing," said Dorcas, "but we can't let them control every minute of our lives ... Cadi, are you listening?"

"I don't know where you get your fancy ideas from. You've never been in service before, have you?"

"No."

Cadi opened a door into a large room then fell to her knees at the fireplace, telling Dorcas to get the ash bucket ready.

"But I do know some who've been in service – and some of them are friends of mine," said Dorcas.

Cadi was concentrating on her work and ignoring her cousin's chat.

"Cadi ..."

Cadi turned to Dorcas. She was frowning.

"Just listen to someone who knows better than you," she said, but in a patient voice. Her expression was more fed up than anything. "Head down, do your work and shut your mouth – that's all you need to do if you want to survive here."

Dorcas remained silent for a long time afterwards. Maybe Cadi wasn't in good form this morning. Maybe she didn't like Dorcas, even if they were related to one another by blood. Maybe she, Dorcas, got on her nerves. Cleaning grates was miserable work – even more miserable was doing it in silence.

Chapter 10

As she cleaned grates, collected soot and swept floors, Dorcas tried to remember what she'd imagined a scullery maid actually did. The truth was she hadn't thought about it a lot. The fact of leaving home had been so frightening that this had been all she could think of. Lisa was a maid in Nannau, but she'd put up with her lot. Of course, life wasn't always a bed of roses for her, but then neither had been Dorcas's life back home – weaving and helping around the house. But, having finished her work for the day, at least Lisa could come home and see her friends. And all the servants and maids were Welsh in Nannau. Here in Penrhyn no one but Cadi could understand her language, and this, together with not being able to go home, caused a terrible loneliness in her.

The constant cleaning and scrubbing was endless and exhausting. Back home, it hadn't been so bad because they only had one fireplace, there weren't many rooms to clean and her mother kept her company as she baked or washed. The children were underfoot, the chickens were outside, people called by ... housework was part and parcel of their day – natural to the pattern of their lives. Dorcas thought now of the times she'd complained of the drudgery of spinning and weaving. At least that work had created something visible and real, even if it was only rough flannel. And it had been work undertaken in the company of her family – it had been something social and quite enjoyable, looking back. In fact, she'd have given anything to be back there again now, carding wool by the fire. She'd never complain about it again in her life.

At the end of her first day in the castle it began to dawn on her how huge was her prison. Having cleaned the fireplaces of ten rooms, and all those in the servants' quarters, she tried to estimate the size of the place. She didn't get the chance to ask Cadi until they got back to their bedroom.

"That's your first day over," Cadi said, removing her cap and placing it on a chair.

"It felt like the longest day in my life! My back's killing me."

Cadi smiled.

"You'll find muscles you didn't know you had. But you're taller than me – you'll adapt very quickly ... Is it what you were expecting?"

Dorcas had to admit that she hadn't thought much about what the work would be like here.

She stretched back on the bed and, glancing at the walls she said,

"Cadi, how many rooms are there in the castle?"

"No idea."

Cadi was in her own little world, tidying her things. Dorcas stared at her.

"But it's you who cleans them."

"I'm just one little maid amongst many," said Cadi, as if reciting a prayer, "and we mostly just work in the servants' quarters."

"I haven't even seen Lord Penrhyn yet," said Dorcas.

Cadi turned to her in astonishment.

"He's not here – that's why," she said, brushing her hair.

"Not here? Where is he then?" asked Dorcas, confused.

"This is just an occasional place for them, a sort of holiday home. Their main home's in London and they've another house somewhere else too. They come and go between the houses, bringing extra staff with them."

Dorcas could hardly believe it. So they were doing all of this work for someone who didn't even live there most of the time!

"And even when they are here, we don't see them," Cadi continued. "They don't want to come into contact with us. They just want us to prepare their food, wash their clothes and clean up after them. In effect, we're invisible. But they're due here next month ... God help us."

"Why?"

"Take it from me. This is the quiet time. The really hectic time hasn't even begun yet."

Dorcas leaned back against the wall.

"How rich is Lord Penrhyn?"

Cadi put down her hair brush.

"Think of the most incredible wealth you can imagine ..."

'Gold from Peru and pearls from faraway India' ... a line from a favourite hymn floated into Dorcas's mind.

"Double it, treble it, and you've some idea of how rich they are. They have more money than people like you and me could ever imagine."

Dorcas got up off the bed and walked to the window. Their

room was on the highest floor and it looked down over the rear of the castle. Dorcas stared out the window, trying to come to terms with what Cadi had just said.

"But how have they got so much money?"

"Who knows? 'Money flows to those who have it' as Mam would say. Lord Penrhyn owns half of Bethesda. He owns the quarry, he owns the inns, he built most of the houses. He owns Llandygái, and he, or his father, built Port Penrhyn, he owns the railway, he owns half of Jamaica ... the man's a money-making machine. Anything he touches turns to gold."

Dorcas thought suddenly of how much Mabli and Lewis would have enjoyed this story, then she remembered she couldn't tell them it and the thought made her despair. And anyway, wasn't there another story about someone who turned everything into gold?

"Look out the window, Dorcas. As far as the horizon. Lord Penrhyn owns all that."

Only in stories had Dorcas heard of such people. To come across a real person with such incredible wealth was something very frightening – and the idea that such a person was actually her employer ...

"I'm not sure if having such wealth is right."

"Why not? Good luck to him – that's all I can say! If it wasn't for the likes of him, the likes of you and me would have no work."

Dorcas continued to stare out through the window.

"But when you think about what it says in the Bible – about the wealthy man ..."

"What does the Bible say about it?" Cadi asked.

"That it's easier for a camel to pass through the eye of a needle than it is for the rich man to enter the Kingdom of Heaven."

Cadi gave a laugh.

"I've never heard that verse before, but it's a funny idea, isn't it?"

Dorcas didn't see what was so funny about it. The idea had never concerned her much before as she hadn't known anyone who was rich – not until now. But if she'd been in Lord Penrhyn's shoes, that verse would have sent shivers down her spine.

"And Jesus Christ says to the wealthy man, 'Sell all that you have, give to the poor and follow me'."

"Where have you learned all this?" Cadi asked.

"At Sunday school. What do you learn there?"

"We don't have Sunday school in church."

Dorcas stared at her cousin, her eyes wide.

"Do you go to the Anglican Church?"

"Yes. That's why I didn't make a fuss about going to the service this morning. Because that's what I'm used to."

Dorcas saw Cadi in a very different light now. She hadn't known any other church people and she'd certainly never talked to one.

"But didn't you know I was a Methodist?" Dorcas asked her cousin.

"I knew – Mam told me. I think that's why our families don't have much to do with each other. Our fathers don't agree on religious matters. But your mam and mine are still friends, and still sisters. Mam told me that I shouldn't bother you about it."

Dorcas went over her cousin's words in her mind, then came over to sit on the bed beside her cousin.

"Does it bother you that I'm a Methodist?"

Cadi shook her head. "I don't know what a Methodist is, to be honest, apart from the fact that they're a stubborn lot. That what Dad says anyway."

"And you don't miss going to Sunday school?"

"I don't know know what you do in Sunday school," Cadi said, fiddling with her dress.

"Well, it's in Sunday school that I learned to read and write, for one thing."

"I can't read much, but I can write my name," said Cadi.

"And at Sunday School we discuss the sermon each week and lessons from the Bible."

Cadi glanced at Dorcas and nodded, as if she was beginning to understand.

"Maybe you shouldn't do that."

"How do you mean?"

"Well, in our church, we don't discuss or debate these questions. We receive the Word of God, and we don't question it."

Dorcas looked at her in confusion as Cadi continued.

"Because, once you begin to question them, things become a source of debate, and nothing good can come of that. You need a boss to tell other people what to do – otherwise, things get all messy."

Dorcas was beginning to understand.

"So, it doesn't bother you that Lord Penrhyn is your boss and everyone else's too ..."

"Why should it bother me? It's just the way the order works, and we all have our place in it."

"But you still find cleaning all day miserable?"

Dorcas was trying her hardest to look for some common ground, but she was to be disappointed.

"Do you know what, Dorcas? I don't think I do. I get up every morning knowing that I have tasks to complete and I'm happy to fulfill my duties, even if I'm exhausted at the end of the day. And when I lay my head down for the night, at least I have the satisfaction of knowing that I've done everything to the best of my ability, and this makes me happy, and I feel like a good girl ... And I remember to say my prayers. You won't go too far wrong if you do the same."

Dorcas stared over at her cousin as if seeing her for the first time.

Cadi got to her feet and began to get ready for bed.

"And I'm glad I'm sharing this room with you, Dorcas. It's really nice to speak Welsh with someone."

Dorcas nodded in agreement. But in the back of her mind, she wondered whether their language was the sole link that bound them.

Chapter 11

Those first few weeks were a confused turmoil of getting to know faces, Dorcas thought as she stared at the bare wall in the little room, turning memories over in her mind. No wonder the first meals in the kitchen had been a real struggle – everyone staring at her and her clueless of all the rules. Over time, she'd learned to tell who was who and where they were from, their names and their role in the castle. Miss Grantham was their boss and then there was a steward, a butler, one or two ladies' maids, the kitchen maids, scullery maids like herself, a valet, a sub-butler, a footman, errand boys, laundry staff, stable lads ... the list was endless. There was a routine to the day, too, and everyone seemed to know where they were supposed to be at what time. At first, Dorcas had thought of them as a swarm of bees, with Miss Grantham as the queen bee, keeping a beady eye over her staff.

Very few of the workers had their own homes. Most of them were tenants on the Penrhyn land, living there only with the permission of the estate. Everyone saw this as the norm and they remained there for life, in most cases. Penrhyn existed for Penrhyn's sake, and many considered serving the estate to be the sole purpose of their existence. The majority of the staff were English. Dorcas could count on one hand how many Welsh people worked there, and she'd made friends with one of them, Hanna.

One afternoon, Dorcas was sent to the kitchen to wash dishes as one of the kitchen staff was unwell, and that's where she met Hanna. Dorcas had never seen such a large kitchen. The huge fireplace dominated the room, with a number of kettles, always on the boil. By the sink was a mountain of dirty dishes waiting to be washed.

"So, have you got your feet under you now?" asked Hanna, washing the dishes as Dorcas dried them.

"I've not fully settled here yet, if that's what you mean."

"You just have to learn how to live here, I suppose. It's difficult to feel at home here."

"Why do they have two kitchens?" asked Dorcas, peeking into an adjoining room.

"That's not a kitchen, it's a pastry room – for making pastries.

"A special room – just to make pastries?"

"Yes," said Hanna, rolling her eyes, "and there's a special room to keep china in, and lamp room to keep lamps in ... There's room for everything under the sun, including a brushing room – to keep brushes."

Dorcas realised that this was the room where she'd spent her first night in the castle.

Hanna carefully placed a giant vegetable dish on the draining board. "Watch that – it's heavy."

Hanna was from Llannefydd near Denbigh, she told Dorcas, and she'd worked for the gentry there. But when one of the maids there had moved to Penrhyn, Hanna had the chance to go with her.

"I thought I'd go up in the world by coming here, but the

opposite happened, to tell you the truth. There was such a large staff here that I was back down at the bottom again. What are you looking at?"

Dorcas had noticed the emblem on the dish.

"I saw this dragon on the front of the castle, and in lots of other places too – is it the family shield?"

"It's not a dragon, but an antelope."

Dorcas looked at Hanna in surprise.

"An antelope? What's that?"

"Something with two horns. I think they're real animals ..."

"Hanna," Dorcas asked, "why is everything so strange here?"

"They're gentry, aren't they – what's to be done?" she answered impatiently.

Then she turned to the stove. "You hungry?" she asked.

Dorcas had been hungry since arriving at the castle.

"Let's finish off what's left in the pan here," Hanna said, putting it on the draining board between them with a grin. "This'll keep us going for a bit."

As Dorcas licked her spoon in satisfaction, Hanna went on, "We're not supposed to do this, but no one'll be the wiser. We're not supposed to use these grand dishes either, but I do sometimes – just for the hell of it ... Look, there's more food over here too."

"Aren't you afraid of losing your job?"

"Come on, Dorcas, it's only a tiny morsel!"

"I've been scared of my shadow since coming here. Cadi keeps telling me I'm far too bold."

"Between you and me," whispered Hanna, "Cadi's a bit of an innocent. We might be maids, but we don't have to be under the thumb every waking moment. Did you know Cadi before coming here?"

"She's my first cousin."

"I'm sorry, I didn't know …"

"Not to worry. Cadi and I hardly know each other. Well, we're getting to know one another now. Where do you sleep?"

"There are three of us at the end of the corridor – me, Harriet and Ada – do you know them? They're English. Harriet's fine, but Ada's a pain. But we all have to live with one another, don't we. Have you heard the Big News?"

"No … Well, maybe they said something and I didn't understand."

"You're having trouble with English, aren't you?"

"We never speak it at home. I've learned 'you lazy Welsh good for nothing' pretty quickly – I've heard it enough times!"

Hanna smiled. She had a warm smile, freckles all over her face and a mop of beautiful red hair to top it off.

"But what's the Big News?"

"The lord's on his way …"

"Here?"

"Well yes! Where else? Wait'll you'll see how the mood here changes in the next week or two. Everyone here will be up to 'high-doh'. It's like a different place once Lord Penrhyn arrives at the castle."

"Will we see him?"

"Not likely. But there's always a lot more work when they're in residence. Nothing you've seen so far compares to it. We never see our beds before midnight."

As she sat in the little room on her own, Dorcas recalled

how she'd felt on hearing this. A mixture of excitement and expectation, and then the fear that she needed to be up to all the work that lay ahead.

"But at least there'll be a purpose to all the slog-work we do around here. Maintaining an empty castle for someone who doesn't live here's a complete waste of time," Hanna had continued. Then she'd added, "But it'll mean much more work for us, a lot more – and Miss Grantham will turn into even more of a lunatic."

As Hanna began emptying the dirty water from the sink she glanced at her hands.

"Look at my poor little hands," she said to Dorcas. "Red-raw and as pink as a lobster ... they're like an old woman's hands. Dear me," and off she went with with the bucket. Dorcas watched her go, straining under its weight. Then Hanna put the bucket down and turned to her.

"Dorcas ..."

"Yes?"

"Did you always imagine that life would be different to this?"

Dorcas looked down at her uniform, at the tea towel in her hand. She didn't really know what to say.

"Well ... I hadn't expected to be a scullery maid in a castle, if that's what you mean. But it's only for the time being, it won't be forever ..."

She saw Hanna watching her. Was it pity she saw in her eyes?

"I remember thinking the same thing when I first came here," said Hanna, before bending to lift the bucket and heading out again.

Dorcas shouted after her.

"And when was that?"

"Five years ago – or is it six now?"

The fact that she couldn't remember made Dorcas's heart sink.

* * *

That evening, Dorcas had time to write a few lines of the letter she'd promised Mabli. She made no mention of the drudgery of cleaning and how strange she felt. She escaped into the world of fantasy, and invented a whole story for Mabli about her new workplace. Penrhyn Castle was extremely grand, with huge golden-coloured gates like the Gates of Heaven. Yes, the work was sometimes monotonous but, come the afternoons, she put on a lace apron and served tea and cake to Lord and Lady Penrhyn. She went into great detail – the stunning designs of Lady Penrhyn's dresses and how beautiful she was. She had three lovely little children and a pet dog called Tomi. Sometimes she even let Dorcas sit on a stool next to her and they'd share a slice of cake. Yes, life at the castle was far better than anything she could ever have imagined. And the funniest thing of all was the yellow-green parrot who lived in a cage in the corner of the parlour.

Dorcas was surprised at how easily these fibs came to her and how much she enjoyed writing the letter, though every word of it was a pure lie.

Chapter 12

What Hanna had said proved true. In three weeks' time, Lord Penrhyn and his family were due to arrive – this meant cleaning the castle, fresh linen in every bedroom, supplies brought in and menus prepared. As soon as the visit was announced, it was all hands to the wheel, and everyone was expected to work every daylight hour.

Cadi and Dorcas were still working together every morning, with Cadi assigning different tasks to Dorcas. Gradually, Dorcas's confidence increased, and she began to understand more English. She still wasn't confident in speaking it, but she wasn't long in picking up the gist of what other people were saying, though she had trouble following a conversation.

That morning, as ever, the two of them climbed the staircase to begin their work, and the lord's visit was the main subject of their conversation. Their first task was to clean the corridor, and each was armed with a broom.

"Hanna told me we won't see the lord and his family."

"Why would you? You're just a lowly maid," Cadi told Dorcas. "Only the higher maids wait on the lord, and he and his family have their own staff anyway."

"Their own staff? Why?"

"They're people they trust, people who're familiar to them ..."

Dorcas put her broom down and looked at her cousin.

"But what's the point of employing us then?"

"We're the dirt at the bottom of the heap, Dorcas. I've already told you. They need people to wait on their servants."

The two girls were silent for while, with Dorcas trying to imagine how it would be to be a servant to other people's servants. Having finished sweeping the corridor they went on to the landing.

"I don't understand, Cadi ..."

"We're not supposed to talk while working, you know that."

"I'm just wondering – the new staff will be staying here too – is there room for them?"

"There's no shortage of room, but it means double the work for us ..." Cadi went to fetch mops and buckets from the broom cupboard and turned to Dorcas. "Will you do the usual rooms? I'll go to the far end and spring-clean the extra rooms." As Cadi hurried away, Dorcas said,

"Cadi?"

"What now, Dorcas? Come on, will you? We need to get cracking."

"What does 'scullery maid' mean? What's a 'scullery'? I've never asked ..."

"It means 'back of the kitchen'. The scullery maid is the lowest of all the maids, close to being a slave." And off she went.

Dorcas didn't feel like a scullery maid. She was Dorcas Edwards from Dolgellau, a young woman with her own skill. She was a weaver who'd learned the craft of spinning yarn and making it into cloth. She'd been sent to work in service to the gentry for a short time while her family faced hard times. But soon, her day of freedom would come and she wouldn't be anyone's scullery maid ever again. She was too clever, too bright and lively.

As she cleared the grate in the third room, it seemed to Dorcas that the morning was dragging on forever and so she began to sing to herself:

"Yn y môr y byddo'r mynydd
Sydd yn cuddio bro Meirionnydd;
Na chawn unwaith olwg arni
Cyn i'm calon dirion dorri ..." [1]

As she sang she swept the last of the soot from the hearth and laid a fire in the grate.

"That's a pretty voice you have," said a man's voice, in English.

Dorcas almost jumped out of her skin, and saw a young servant coming towards her with a scuttle of coal.

"Here's the coal. Sorry I'm late. I'm Frank ... you're the new one, aren't you?"

Dorcas had no idea what he was saying.

"Good day," she said, assuming that this meant 'hello'.

"All right, I'll be going, don't worry. I was just trying to be friendly." He sounded disappointed, and he strode out

---

[1] "The mountain, she joins the sea,
She conceals the face of Merioneth,
Let me see her once again
Before my tender heart is broken ..."

through the door again, leaving Dorcas wondering what she'd done wrong. She didn't sing for the rest of that morning.

The rest of the staff showed very little sympathy with her lack of English.

One evening, when she had a few spare minutes, she'd been reading in the kitchen next to Cadi. One of the kitchen staff, Harriet, came in.

"Good Lord, I've seen it all now," she said, looking at Dorcas. "How come you can read?"

Dorcas stared at her, and Harriet turned to Cadi.

"What's wrong with her? Is she a mute or what?"

Dorcus could reply for herself. "No much English," she said.

But Harriet was still looking at Cadi.

"What's she trying to say?"

Cadi jumped to her rescue. "Her English is a bit rusty, that's all. She's all there."

"She's very smart if she can read. Can you write as well?"

"Yes, swell," said Dorcas.

"Can't make head nor tail of what she's saying, poor lass! Anyway, hope you're settling in, girl."

Dorcas smiled at her as she left, but Cadi felt awkward.

"That was embarrassing, Dorcas. You'll have to learn more English. They don't think you're the full nine yards."

The daily church service wasn't much help in learning English. The priest's voice was as monotonous as the buzzing of bees, and Dorcas had trouble keeping awake sometimes. The only good thing about the church was that it was a rare opportunity to sit down and rest. Dorcas used the time to remember her family and hope they were all well. She stared at the babies with wings that were painted on the walls and wondered what they were. She'd never seen a baby angel before. They reminded her of Deio. The following day after church, Cadi told Dorcas they'd been instructed to clean the living rooms in the lord's part of the castle. With their arms full of cleaning gear, Dorcas followed her cousin, feeling a sense of excitement. Apart from going to church, Dorcas hadn't seen this half of the castle. The size of the rooms astonished her, until they reached the hall.

She stood there, stock-still, as if she'd just been struck by a magic wand.

"Are you all right, Dorcas?"

Dorcas had just stepped into a magical world. The sight of it stole her breath. She'd never seen anything like it in her life. She might almost have been outside in the fresh air, the room was so big. But it wasn't a room, it was the heart of the castle, with ways leading off in all sorts of directions. The ceiling stretched to the heavens. Dorcas couldn't see any walls before her either, but carved pillars, soaring up before her eyes. Between the pillars there were all sorts of hidden pathways and places. The windows that faced her were three times, four times bigger than the average door, and above them was another row of windows, all made of stained glass. In her wildest dreams, Dorcas could never have imagined anything so beautiful and full of grandeur. What in the world would Mabli say? Above, the gallery's colonnade revealed an equally splendid second floor.

Dorcas followed the pillars up with her eyes, trying to take in every detail. The work was so intricate, it was as if someone had carved the designs into butter. How was it possible to carve such shapes out of stone? How long would it have taken the stonemasons? Surely the *tylwyth teg*, the fair people, had done this work ...

"Dorcas?"

There was one surprise after another, and her head was spinning. The pillars were topped by faces – a magical lion's head, the devil's head, the head of a goblin – all staring at her and sniggering slyly. What secrets did they know?

And the ceiling! Brilliant white, with a round window at its centre, with the light of heaven shining eerily through it. The ceiling itself was covered in carvings, pattern on pattern, and all as intricate as lace. It was completely, completely incredible.

"Dorcas?"

"I've never seen anywhere like this in my life ..."

"Your mouth's gaping like a fish! I thought for a moment you'd had a stroke ... Come on."

"What is this room?"

"It's called the Great Hall. It's a sort of entrance hall leading to other rooms. Dorcas – come on! We're supposed to start in the drawing room, but you need to snap out of it first ... I'm well used to it now, but I think I was as shocked as you the first time I saw it."

Cadi opened the door to another huge room where everything was covered in dust sheets.

"The first thing we have to do is take off the dust sheets – they're heavy, I'm warning you now," Cadi sighed. "There's so much work to do. We have to dust as much as we can, then the other maids will do the rest. Dorcas, are are you listening?"

"It looks funny, doesn't it? Like monsters or giant tortoises are having a nap under the sheets ..."

Cadi looked at her.

"You have a strange imagination. That thought would never have crossed my mind. Right – grab this corner."

That's how they spent the rest of that afternoon – pulling off dust sheets and carrying them outside to shake. Dorcas breathed in the fresh air, enjoying herself.

"Oh, it's good to be outside, Cadi. It must be three weeks since since I've been outside, apart from crossing the courtyard. Back home, I was out every day, in the fields or going down to town. I miss the freedom of it ..."

"And where would you go from here if you had the chance? Llandygái has only about nine houses, and Bangor must be two miles away. Sure, we're in the middle of nowhere."

"I wouldn't care where I went as long as I wasn't locked up in this castle."

"But you were blathering on about how wonderful it was just now," said Cadi, unable to understand.

"It's an amazing place, but I feel like a prisoner here," explained Dorcas.

"I think you fancy yourself a bit as a bit of a lady," Cadi said, in such a humourless way that Dorcas wasn't sure whether she was pulling her leg or not. "You'd like to be taking tea then taking a ride down to the park in a horse and carriage ..."

"I should be delighted to do that," replied Dorcas, sinking into one of the plush chairs.

Cadi's eyes grew as big as saucers, and her face paled.

"Don't, Dorcas! Get up this minute! You're not supposed to touch the furniture!"

Dorcas jumped to her feet as if the chair was on fire.

"All right! I was only sitting down ..."

"Don't ever do it again," Cadi said breathlessly. "If Miss Grantham were to see you, that would be it for you."

"'You lazy Welsh good for nothing' – yes, yes, I know." Dorcas recalling what Hanna had said about Cadi, about how she was scared of her own shadow.

Under every dust sheet they discovered one treasure after the next. A table made of French hazelwood, an elaborately carved fireplace, graceful candlesticks, a mirror the size of a wall. With feather dusters, the two of them pulled down the worst of the spider webs, but their backs ached sorely by tea-time.

"I wonder if the spiders know they're living in a grand place?" asked Dorcas.

"What?"

"Everything else is so grand here," said Dorcas. "I wonder if even the spiders are high-brow. Do they think they're better than other spiders because they live in one of the grandest rooms in the land?"

"I've never thought about it," said Cadi. A spider was a spider to her, and they all had to go.

Chapter 13

Of all the time she been at the castle, it was those three weeks of preparation for the arrival of Lord Penrhyn that Dorcas enjoyed the most. Cleaning the rooms was exhausting work but discovering so many new and wonderful treasures every day gave her a thrill. The only thing that spoilt it was the way that Cadi kept a constant eye on her.

"I can dust without you watching me," snapped Dorcas one morning while they were working in the drawing room.

Cadi sighed.

"I've never seen anyone so slow to learn as you. I've been doing this work for years – maybe I know more about it than you ..."

"I've had enough experience with mops and brooms too, you know."

The slow way that Dorcas set about tasks got under Cadi's skin and Dorcas, in her turn, was sensitive to criticism.

"I'm scared in case you break something – some things here are so delicate and valuable." Cadi really was anxious.

Dorcas stopped dusting and turned to her.

"I promise to be careful, Cadi. But an accident is an accident – if one should happen. Don't be so worried, for goodness' sake. If something gets broken, they can easily afford another – it's not as if the family are short of a bob or two."

Though Dorcas hadn't meant to sound mean, Cadi exploded.

"That's exactly what makes me nervous!" she cried, and her eyes, that were usually so dull, flashed with anger. "You don't know what these things are worth! 'Buy another one!' indeed. The furniture here's worth hundreds and hundreds of pounds. One small scratch, and it loses its value. I just don't know what to do with you!" She was almost in tears.

At that very moment, they heard the sound of footsteps approaching the room, and a face appeared in the doorway. It was Miss Grantham.

"Quiet, girls! You shouldn't be talking at all, let alone raising your voices."

She looked at Cadi. "Whatever's the matter? Is this one giving you trouble?"

"No, Miss Grantham. I've a bad toothache and it's causing me distress."

Miss Grantham turned to Dorcas. "Why are you staring at me like a goldfish?"

"Good day, Miss Grantham," said Dorcas.

"Oh Edwards, haven't you got beyond 'Good Day' yet? I thought you were supposed to be teaching her, Kadi?"

"Yes, miss."

"Proper mountain goat, this one. I hope her cleaning skills are better than her English."

"Sorry, Miss Grantham," said Dorcas.

"Just make sure she's careful, Kadi, that's all I'm telling you. You're both in a position of trust – and you need to step up – you're falling behind schedule."

And off she went like a ship in full sail.

The two maids looked at one another.

"I'm sorry, Cadi. I'll try to be more careful ..."

Dorcas knew that arguing with Cadi was a very foolish thing to do. If she fell out with Cadi, she'd be completely on her own.

"Hopefully you can see now why I'm so anxious."

"Yes. Sorry. What are 'toothache' and 'distress'?"

"Dannodd." Cadi translated.

"Have you got a toothache?"

"No, but I had to think of some excuse, didn't I?"

"Thank you, Cadi."

So it was that Dorcas wound Cadi up, and Cadi's careful nature made Dorcas bristle. But as the weeks passed, they learned to co-exist and Dorcas's English gradually got better. She still had trouble following a conversation when more than one person was speaking, but she was fine when people spoke slowly and patiently.

When Dorcas first entered the dining room to clean it, she couldn't believe her eyes. It was a room fit for a king. She couldn't take her eyes off the ceiling with its intricate decorations, every one of which was perfect. The enormous dining table practically filled the room and was polished so brilliantly that you could see your face in it. Each of the chairs shone too, and the carpet was luxurious underfoot. Just being in the room for a few minutes made Dorcas feel like a different person. Hanna was working alongside her today and they were cleaning the brass.

"You really love this room, don't you?" Hanna said.

"I still can't believe a place like this exists. Look – the table's so shiny!"

"When the candlesticks are all lit, it's even more magical. A bit of polish on them will transform them too. We'll need to put a canvas over the table first – they're too heavy for us to carry down to the cellar."

Dorcas went over to stare at the giant portrait that covered the wall at the far end of the room.

"So this is them, then?" she asked, examining the family group of father, mother and six children.

"Hmm … those are the lord's parents, I think. I like the dogs best, they look so lifelike."

It all looked lifelike to Dorcas. She'd never seen such a picture before, especially one as enormous as this. Their clothes were magnificent and luxurious-looking and one of the daughters had a large bird on her arm.

"So the lord must be one of these children, then?"

"Yes – not the eldest, the one in red, but the one next to him – the one with his hand on the greyhound. He built this castle. His father died about fifteen years ago."

Dorcas stared at the privileged child in the picture. It was strange to think that this was the present-day Lord Penrhyn. He looked too innocent to be the lord.

"Who are the others in these pictures?" she asked, looking around at all the other portraits in their fine frames.

"I've no idea – probably other family members. They all look the same to me."

"Well, of course they would, they're all related to each other," said Dorcas. "And if I owned a room like this, I'd love to have a picture of Dad and Mam there, and Ifan and Mabli and ..."

She couldn't say their names, she missed them so much. She realised that she never said their names – because no one here knew them.

Come on, let's get started," said Hanna, to cover this sudden awkwardness. "Or before we know it it'll be tea-time, and we'll have done nothing."

When Cadi arrived later to help them finish the room, she was pleased to see that everything looked so good.

"Cadi, did you know that this was the lord when he was a little boy?" Dorcas said, pointing to the painting.

Cadi looked at it.

"Dorcas wants to get acquainted with them," said Hanna, teasingly. She was taking a break from polishing.

"Yes, that's George," she said. "He's old now. But everyone calls him Lord Penrhyn."

Dorcas was still polishing her candlestick. "Except for his wife, I expect," she said. "She'd call him George."

"His wife died," explained Cadi, putting the polished brass on the table. "She was Lady Sophia. But then he remarried."

"I told you she was good at family history, didn't I?" said Hanna. "They all look the same to me."

"Did Lady Sophia have children?" asked Dorcas. To her, they were like the characters in a story.

"Yes, two girls, but they're young ladies by now. Juliana something is the eldest ... Juliana Isabella – that's it! And the youngest is Emma Elizabeth. They're very close together in age."

"Grand names, aren't they?" said Hanna. "How would you fancy being called Dorcas Isabella?" Hanna had no interest whatsoever in the family.

"They're known as the Slate Queens," Cadi continued. "Juliana is 'the Queen of Diamonds', and the other one is 'the Queen of Hearts'."

"Can they speak Welsh?"

"Are you crazy, Dorcas?" snapped Cadi. "They're staunch Englishwomen. Lord Penrhyn's a member of the English Parliament. What use would Welsh be to him?"

Dorcas felt foolish. She'd just wanted to know.

"I just thought that because he was brought up here he might have some grasp of the language."

Hanna watched the two of them with interest. She didn't care two hoots about the lord, but this discussion was interesting. It was obvious that Dorcas was a clever girl.

"He didn't know anything about the castle until he inherited it," Cadi explained. "How would he know about a place like this when he was living in faraway England?"

"But his surname is Pennant, isn't it?" argued Dorcas. She knew that much. "And that's a Welsh name."

"He just stuck Pennant onto his name."

Dorcas didn't know that people could do that.

Cadi continued, "A gentleman named Richard Pennant died and he had no heir, so his title had to be passed onto someone else. This George was related to him somehow – don't ask me how – another branch of the family, so he ended up inheriting Penrhyn. George Hay Dawkins Pennant ... that's his full name."

"Think of the shock," said Hanna, who was polishing again now. "Getting a letter one morning saying: 'You have inherited Penrhyn Castle.'"

"It wasn't much of a castle in those days. This building's just one of the present lord's whims. It was always a fine building but nothing compared to what it is now. He's just keeps adding to it all the time," said Cadi.

"So the castle isn't old?" asked Dorcas.

"No. It just looks old."

Why would you build something new but try to make it look old? Dorcas wondered. Everything about this place was odd.

"Why would you do that?"

"What else do you do when you have so much money?" asked Hanna. "You have to spend it somehow."

"But he doesn't even live here," said Dorcas. "That's a bigger mystery than anything."

"Who knows how these gentry people think? They don't think the same way as us," said Hanna philosophically.

By now Cadi had finished tidying the room.

"But Dorcas has a point, Hanna. If he puts all that money into this place, you'd expect him to spend more time living here, wouldn't you? So the other homes he owns must be just as grand as this one."

As she stood on a stool to try to reach a cobweb, Dorcas noticed two paintings the likes of which she'd never seen before. They were from a faraway country with huge cliffs and a river in the foreground. On either side of the river, black people were working at different tasks.

Dorcas had never seen black-skinned people before.

"These are the strangest pictures I've ever seen – have you noticed them?" she asked the other girls.

Hanna came over. "Those are pictures from Jamaica, for sure."

"Has Lord Penrhyn travelled that far, then?"

"Travelled there?" said Cadi. "He owns the place."

Dorcas looked at her in confusion, and Cadi turned to Hanna.

"Better not tell her anything about Lord Penrhyn's wealth. She's got no idea."

"I don't understand," said Dorcas. "If he owns so much land in this country, why does he need more in Jamaica?"

"Slaves," said Cadi, as if it was completely obvious. "He has labourers making money for him in the quarry, us working for him here, and slaves making money for him on the other side of the world."

Dorcas stared at the picture for a long time. So these were the slaves. Here were their clothes. It was for these people that her family had spun and woven all that cloth. Until now, they'd been like characters in an imaginary story. Strange to see them in the middle of their own land. And they were so small in this picture that you couldn't see their faces. So different to the painting of the lord's family

Dorcas examined the other picture – a quiet rural scence with a large houses in the background. There were four oxen and a cart in a field, with slaves standing around them. They didn't look as if they were suffering too badly. She could see that they were cutting hay with scythes. The grass was tall and green. What caught her eye then took her breath away. The clothes they were wearing were bright blue, purple and red. She'd been right all along! Dying the yarn before weaving the cloth, families like hers would've been able to make more profit on them. And to think that Ifan had been so dismissive of her idea.

"Is the place in order now?" asked Hanna. "I'm starving."

Cadi scanned the room. "Yes. I think even Miss Grantham would be satisfied with this."

"Dorcas, are you finished staring at those pictures yet?"

"I'm coming!" said Dorcas, hurrying to join the others.

Chapter 14

Lord Penrhyn's family arrived in the end, after all the hullabaloo of preparations. For Dorcas and the other maids, it was as if the Day of Judgement was upon them. Miss Grantham and the head-staff had worked themselves into panic like no other. After seeing one of paintings in the castle's finest rooms, Dorcas wondered how they'd arrive – perhaps a golden carriage would appear through the clouds with little angels playing trumpets in celebration. When word reached them that the lord's family were here, Dorcas and the other maids rushed to the window at the top of the castle to watch the show.

Even now, Dorcas was surprised to see the size of the cavalcade. In no time the castle courtyard had filled with half a dozen horses and carriages and the atmosphere changed at once. Most incredible of all – to Dorcas's mind – were the splendid outfits the girls were wearing. They looked incredible – so elegant and well-groomed, each of them, with small, dainty bonnets. They looked just like little china dolls. The senior staff at Penrhyn stood in a row and formed a guard of honour to welcome them, while the courtyard swarmed with people unloading cases and boxes from the carriages and carts, shaking hands and unhitching the horses. Dorcas was captivated by the busy scene and all its comings and goings.

"How many of them are there?" she asked in wonder.

"Enough to make sure we'll be on our knees in no time," Cadi said peevishly. "You'll be praying to see the back of them again in a while, believe me. I don't know what you're so excited about."

But Dorcas couldn't help herself. Finally, something was happening to break the monotony. Finally, they'd be under the same roof as these Very Important People. What would Mabli have made of all of this? She'd have loved every moment of it.

"You won't meet any of them, you know that," said Sybil, another of the maids.

"Is that true, Cadi?" asked Dorcas quietly.

"Yes – I've told you before. You're not important enough. None of us are. Just imagine you're a cockroach or a woodlouse, scuttling about in fear of being trodden on. That's what we'll be for the next few weeks."

Dorcas would have good reason to recall Cadi's words.

Later, imprisoned in the small, stark room and contemplating her life so far, Dorcas thought that this was when things had really gone awry. Yes, she'd been unhappy, but she'd been able to tolerate things and she could keep going from day to day. Misery had typified those first few weeks, and her inability to speak English.

But the arrival of Lord Penrhyn and his family turned life in the castle upside down, and nothing was the same afterwards. But why should that surprise her? That was what lords had done right down the ages.

Dorcas had worked hard, had done her best, but her best hadn't been good enough. She'd begun to sink, and nothing now could save her.

She thought of how she'd marvelled at all the wonders in

those luxurious rooms during the first few weeks. She hadn't believed before that such beauty could exist. Should she have seen this as a warning sign? After all, what kind of people would hoard such a vain and frivolous collection? Every day had revealed a fantasy more wonderful than the day before, and her imagination had been set afire. Even though she'd been working hard to prepare for the lord's arrival, seeing such ornaments in such rooms had been a daily pleasure. It had opened her mind to things to refinement and beauty.

And she'd got to know Cadi and Hanna better. To all intents and purposes, Dorcas had begun to settle into her new environment.

But hadn't Cadi warned her? Cadi had told her more than once that this was the calm before the storm. And when the storm came, it had come like a hurricane and torn her life into tiny pieces. And that was why she was now alone in a room the size of a box, waiting her sentence.

The fact that they didn't see the visitors was the strangest thing of all. The castle became two places – one half as busy as an ants' nest while the other half grew fat on their labour. The distinctions made between the lord's own private domestic staff and the staff that worked there all year round was the biggest bone of contention, and created a great deal of tension throughout the castle. Dorcas never thought that she'd have much sympathy for Miss Grantham, never mind that her authority would be undermined, and that she'd be seen as inferior to the next group. This change in the organization of the castle staff meant having to understand a different chain of command – more faces and more hierarchies. Even on the lowest rung of servants and maids, on Dorcas's level, they were still at the bottom, they had to follow orders.

There was trouble with the new staff from the first day. A large group of them had accompanied Lord Penrhyn's family to the castle and they had their own systems and structures, different from the staff already working there. The new staff considered themselves superior and were treated as such by the lord's family. They spoke the best English and were given the most important jobs. And they completely destroyed the routine that everyone was used to as relating to the castle's kitchens. Their chef took over the kitchen, and Miss Grantham had to accede to all of their instructions and requests. Lord Penrhyn had his own butler and his footmen, and all of the usual staff of the castle were demoted in the hierarchy upon his arrival. Once everyone was made aware of their standing in the new set-up, Dorcas thought that things would settle down, but this wasn't the case. Misunderstandings continued with regard to who was responsible for what, and people continued to pull rank on others. Cadi and Dorcas's daily tasks did not include included cleaning the big rooms any more; they were relegated to cleaning the kitchens, doing the beds and the looking after the fires. But now that they were on-duty almost constantly, the month that Lord Penrhyn and his family were there proved more exhausting than anything Cadi and the others had ever known. It was never clear to them when their duties were completed for the day.

"I can't do any more," said Dorcas one night after a long day. "I'm falling asleep standing up."

Cadi stared at her cousin.

"Well, this is going to be interesting. Are you going on strike, Dorcas? We've never had a strike in the castle before! What do you think we should do?"

"What do you mean?" asked Dorcas.

"Stop working – it happened in the slate quarry five years ago, according to Father. The quarrymen workers stayed away from work for one full day because they wanted better terms and conditions. Greedy sods."

"Don't go on, Cadi."

"Can you remember these English words, 'I'm not working any more', can you?" Cadi mocked her cousin further.

It was better to ignore her.

"I only said I was tired," Dorcas said. "I'm just so tired, I can barely move ..."

They were sitting in the kitchen at that point and the clock had just turned ten o'clock at night. They'd just finished washing up after supper for everyone in the castle, and they were all completely exhausted. Lord Penrhyn and his family were still awake and the other servants were still busy serving them. The scullery maids and all of the kitchen staff weren't permitted to leave and to go to bed until the kitchen was completely cleared for the next day. This was an enormous kitchen and in a matter of a few hours, come early dawn, Dorcas and the others would be back working there again at the start of another day.

Miss Grantham came in through the door, unannounced.

"Well, well, this is a pretty picture," she said sarcastically. "Two lazy Welsh goats already sitting down for the night."

Cadi jumped to her feet and apologised.

"Edwards, get up!" Miss Grantham barked.

Dorcas felt her head spin as she got to her feet.

"I'm very tired, Miss Grantham."

"Well, listen girl, you better get used to this, as this is how things are going to be for the next few months. The lord loves his evening tipple. He loves entertaining. And you're not dismissed for the evening until he's finished. Wait until the last of the dishes come in and make sure everything is washed clean and spotless. This kitchen has to be spick and span first thing tomorrow morning. I'm retiring for the night now. Good night," she said, "and shut the door."

The door was closed.

"Never tell Grantham you're tired, Dorcas. She sees it as a sign of weakness. Dorcas! Dorcas! Are you listening to me?"

But Dorcas had already fallen back on the chair and was fast asleep.

Chapter 15

If Dorcas had thought of the bed as a form of escape that
night, she was very wrong. She and Cadi had barely drifted off
to sleep in their room high upstairs around about midnight
when she heard the sound of somone sobbing and weeping.

"Cadi ... Cadi ... what's the matter?"

Dorcas got up and went over to Cadi who was in a heavy
sleep. Maybe she'd imagined whatever it was. Dorcas went
back to bed and tried to settle again, but just as she was about
to fall asleep, she heard the same sound. She jumped up,
thinking there was someone in the room.

"Who's there?" she whispered.

She listened. Yes, someone was definitely crying, but the
noise was outside rather than inside the room. She tiptoed
over to the bedroom door. Even if leaving the room during
the night was forbidden, she couldn't ignore that
heartwrenching sound. She turned the door handle. It was so
dark that Dorcas could barely see but she ventured out
barefoot into the corridor, although was uncertain where she
was going. It was difficult to tell where the noise had come
from. She stopped momentarily. Nothing but the sound of
her own heart beating. Maybe she was imagining things,
Dorcas thought. Was she losing her mind? Was the noise real
or was it a sign or a warning of some description? Maybe
someone at home was sick? Was her father ill?

The sound came again, weaker this time. It was more like a sigh. Maybe she wasn't supposed to hear this sound, whatever it was. Maybe she'd be better off minding her own business. But it was a heartwrenching noise – it sounded like some poor creature needed help. She crept her way slowly along the corridor and spotted a shadow. She froze.

Whatever it was, she wasn't supposed to see it. She turned on her heels and hurried back to her room, her heart hammering in fright. She crawled back beneath the covers but there was no way she could get back to sleep. She twisted and turned in her in the bed for ages, and in the end, went over to the window. A moon like a wheel hung high in the sky, a moon so bright it lit up the darkness. Dorcas found it comforting to think that it was this same moon that her sister Mabli could see if she peered out through her bedroom window in Tyddyn Priciau at that same moment. But Mabli was probably tucked up in her bed, sleeping soundly. There was nothing romantic in the pale moonlight for Dorcas any longer – all of her dreams had disappeared on the long journey from Betws-y-coed on that first ever night she'd left home. Dorcas returned to bed, and eventually, even if it was a few hours later, sleep came and her worries were forgotten.

Dawn came around far too quickly and a weary Dorcas struggled to face another day, only waking after Cadi's constant promptings. Dorcas didn't say anything to Cadi about what she'd heard the previous night, as she knew her cousin would just make fun of her if she did. Cadi would have told her to have a bit of sense – that the sounds were surely just the work of her imagination. Although it was still only five o'clock in the morning, they had to dress and wash and make their beds.

The first task of the day was to get the kitchen stove going again and rekindle the cinders left from the previous night.

"I sometimes feel it's not worth our while going to bed at all," Cadi said. "Your head has barely hit the pillow before it feels like time to get up again. You were right last night about that, Dorcas. We might as well have slept down here, one of us on either side of the hearth, for all the difference it makes climbing up those flights of stairs to sleep in a soft bed." She looked at her cousin.

"Are you alright, Dorcas? You're not sick, are you?"

"No. Just a bit tired," she replied.

The other maids came into the kitchen and began preparing breakfast for all of the servants. Once the stoves were lit, Dorcas had to go back upstairs to all the bedrooms in order to empty out all the chambermaids' pots from the previous night. Unsurprisingly, this was the job that Dorcas hated the most. Once the pots were emptied, they were all scrubbed clean with cloths and vinegar until you could see your face in them. This was one job she would never get used to, no doubt about it. From the corner of her eye, she saw Miss Grantham watching her like a hawk.

"Remember, Edwards – clean as a whistle now. Spotless, that's the way we want them. No cutting corners, mind!"

What a silly thing to say, Dorcas had thought, taking Miss Grantham's words literally. There were no corners on a piss-pot anyway, were there?

Once she'd completed this task, she had to serve cups of

tea to the servants and the senior house maids and house staff, a job that the newest arrivals always had to do. Such were the highlights of her every morning, Dorcas thought to herself – serve the other staff and fill their tea-cups and then empty their piss-pots! If dreamy Mabli could only see her then, looking after all the servants' needs – serving everyone other than herself. The routine was all designed to make you learn your place in the pecking order and to know how powerless and inferior you really were within the hierarchy of that house. The latest command was that she was to curtsy the head chef.

Dorcas's major task this morning was to help the head chef in the kitchen with all of his breakfast orders. There was no time for a bite to touch her own lips and Dorcas shook her head in despair. If her parents had known what life was really like in this place, would they have let her go so easily and encouraged her to leave home so young? Or was it becase that they couldn't take her home again – that they simply couldn't support her? Had they known that attendance at this church daily was obligatory, for fear or punishment, might they have thought differently? Dorcas hadn't written another letter home to Mabli following her first one, full of fibs and lies. After just a few weeks in the castle, she'd felt herself changing, her youthful joy slipping away from her to be replaced by the hardness and a bitterness that characterised the daily routine.

* * *

Dorcas, Cadi and the other maids were given a quarter of an hour to eat whatever food they could lay their hands on, once everyone else in the castle had been fed. Breakfast over, it was time to clear up after the rest of the maids and the servants, and wash all of their breakfast dishes and cutlery. Carrying water to the stove and heating it until it boiled was Dorcas's main task following breakfast. It was heavy work and a big strain on her shoulders, her back and her legs. She was glad that Mabli wasn't given the chance to work with her. Wasn't Mabli lucky that she was still too young to do such work? The only break was in church during the morning service where you could rest for a short half-hour or so.

Washing the back floor of the scullery before lunch, Dorcas had a chance to chat with Hanna.

"You look terrible, Dorcas."

To her surprise, Dorcas had burst out crying and couldn't stop, the tears streaming down her face. Hanna wrapped her arms around her and gave her a hug to try and comfort her.

"What in the world is wrong, Dorcas dear? What's come over you, love?"

"I don't know, to tell you the truth ... It's just that I'm tired ... so tired, that's all," she said, still weeping.

"Have you been getting enough sleep? If you don't sleep right, you won't be long falling sick, Dorcas. You have to mind yourself. Only the toughest survive here, you know."

For a brief moment, Dorcas thought of telling her about the strange and pitiful voice calling out in the darkness the previous night, but she quickly recovered heself. It would sound ridiculous, she thought. And they'd only think that she was light in the head.

"I was in bed by midnight but I just couldn't sleep ... too

many thoughts running through my mind," sobbed Dorcas.

"But crying like this is not like you at all, girl? What is it?"

"I know, I know. It's just that I've reached the end of my tether."

It was a relief to sit down on the kitchen floor for a moment and to unburden herself to someone else – to let it all out.

"Take a break for a minute. That old Grantham's minions won't be around here checking on us for a while yet. But I'd better keep going here for the time being, just in case."

Hanna really was an angel from heaven, Dorcas thought. Not all the other maids were bad people – it was just that she couldn't talk to them in their own language yet, as her knowledge of English was still very limited. It was thinking of Ifan and Mabli and little Lewis at home without her that really broke her heart. She missed them so much and felt so lonely without them.

"Did something happen to you, Dorcas?" Hanna asked, but Dorcas shook her head.

"I just feel very lonely, that's all."

Hanna understood how much loneliness could affect someone. It was something that caused terrible pain – body and soul.

"I know what you mean, Dorcas. I felt the same way as you when I first went into service. There's nothing more terrible than being separated from your family. It's like a hole inside you that nothing and nobody can fill. And it stays with you all the time, this *hiraeth*, like a great hurt that just won't go away. All you can do is learn to live with it … there's no escaping it."

"And … and … I'm so hungry, so weak. I should have some

food – it's just that I can't bring myself to eat anything," Dorcas whimpered.

Hanna went out to the kitchen and returned with a cup of water and a slice of bread.

"Here you go!" she said. "I know that a cup of tea would be a better idea, but I'll be in trouble if I get caught bringing that to you," she said, handing Dorcas a slice and eating the other slice herself.

"But we can't eat this ... can we?" said Dorcas anxiously.

"Take it, take what you can and no one will be any the wiser. For God's sake, girl, you're hungry and weak and we're working in a kitchen! What else should someone do? The gentry were up late last night having a good time, and they'll be expecting us to have a big lunch ready for them as soon as they wake up – you wait and see. I've no time for them. They're like rich spoilt dogs, and us waiting on them hand and foot, all day and half the night. Now eat this quickly before anyone finds out."

Dorcas obeyed, secretly admiring Hanna's rebellious spirit. She had more fire in her belly, whereas Cadi was as quiet and calm as a lake in good weather.

Hanna got to her feet and went over to the corner of the room where there were two buckets.

"Right so, how are you feeling now? Are you feeling a bit better?"

Dorcas nodded.

"Now, let's go outside and bring the potatoes in. Some fresh air will do you good. I know it's not your job officially, Dorcas – my back and legs are sore but I better get up,"

Hanna said, pretending to be an old woman, turning to Dorcas and smiling. "I'm having trouble moving and bending my back, I think I'm getting old already," Hanna said. "Soon I'll need help filling sacks of potatoes and bringing them in, and I know you won't let an old one like me down ..." she said, winking. Dorcas gave a wry smile in return.

"Alright, I'll come with you."

"You see? My plan worked! And I've put a smile on your face at the same time ..."

"Thank you, Hanna, for being so kind to me. You're such a tonic. We'll have to keep an eye out for Grantham's brown noses and spies while we're at it." The girls went outside to the gardens and into the byre where the potatoes were piled up.

"Grantham's minions won't find us. They have plenty of other people to hassle. Don't worry ..."

The girls had a good ten minutes out the back in the fresh air, filling the sacks with new potatoes. Miss Grantham and her gang never bothered them.

Chapter 16

What did Lord Penrhyn's family do all day long while they were staying at the castle? This was a question that went through Dorcas's mind regularly in those first few weeks. They liked to spend hours and hours in their beds sleeping and even eating their food between the covers, sometimes. Then, once they felt like it, they spent the rest of the morning getting dressed up in the grandest of clothes and decorating their hair in the finest of tresses and braids. After lunch, what was there to do? They didn't have to clean up after themselves as they had so many servants to do this on their behalf; neither had they any washing or laundry duties. All they need do was drop the clothes they'd worn onto the ground and there were others to pick up after them. What a strange existence – nothing to do for hours on end. How on earth did they fill their time?

Dorcas knew the answer – entertaining! They all spent every evening feasting and drinking to excess, but what else was there to do? Did such a life of luxury become boring and empty eventually, in the absence of any real work? Wasn't there something hollow about such an existence after all? Dorcas wondered. She knew that she hated idleness and indolence herself, even if she complained about her exhaustion at the end of every day. Sooner or later, she'd have to send another letter home, a letter in which she'd tell Mabli the truth. She'd tell her sister how she'd started to change her mind about the games which the 'idle rich' played. Her sweet sister may have longed to live such a life, but maybe it was a mirage or an illusion … If only Mabli knew what such an existence was really like!

The fact that they so rarely saw Lord Penrhyn's family in the flesh was one of the strangest aspects of all, especially given that they were all under the one roof in the castle. It was easy to believe that these gentry were just figments of the imagination, that they weren't really there at all.

The dirt they left behind them was clear to everyone, however. It was proof enough of their day-to-day lives. Tons of food would leave the kitchen, and a whole slew of dirty plates and glasses came back again. The gentry drank heavily – like fish – as evident from the piles of empty wine bottles at the end of every night. They produced a constant stream of dirty laundry, so that the servants were busy all day long washing and airing. They regularly left their muddy shoes and boots outside their rooms for the servants to clean, and in addition to their dirty plates and cutlery, their dirt was the only sign of of their existence.

Dorcas imagined them as invisible creatures whose shoes were the only things the human eye could see. In her imagination, the owners of those shoes almost assumed the status of mythological creatures. The same was true of their underwear drying on the line in the breeze outdoors, as if a host of invisible characters lined up in unison, their underclothes as the sole proof of their existence – the luxurious petticoats of Isabella and Emma Juliana … whatever their names were – and George's collection of socks into the bargain, those that the lord himself sported.

One day Dorcas found herself by one of the windows on the second floor, looking out. In the distance, she saw three men galloping across the fields at speed on their horses. The men were shouting to one another and their mounts were really beautiful, even if they seemed as small figures in the distance. The men all looked so noble and grand in their spurs and finery. They were out hunting, enjoying the excitement of the chase and the hunt, a sport which filled many hours of their lives.

A few nights later, Dorcas was in bed, exhausted after her day's work, when she heard what sounded like weeping and groaning again. What a sad and haunting sound – it was terrible! Yes, that was the sound, the same as the one she'd heard before. She was fully awake and sitting up in the bed. No, she hadn't imagined it after all. There was something louder and more high-pitched about it this time, and she couldn't have ignored it even if she'd tried. She listened carefully again. Someone was in trouble or in pain. Quietly, she got out of bed and went to open the door. It was pitch-black in the corridor outside. The sound went quiet ... nothing, no voice ... and yet ... Yes, there it was again, a low crying, the sound of someone whimpering, far away.

The sound grew louder. It was coming from somewhere in the depths of the castle, a low and frightened moan of despair that cut right through you. What should she do? Wake up Cadi? But then, would Cadi be thankful to her if she shook her awake? She might tell Dorcas to mind her own business, to toughen up ... Whatever it was, it was nothing to do with her. And maybe Cadi was right, maybe she did need to toughen up ... in every way. Life was hard and you had to get used to it. Only the hardest and most resilient survived. Dorcas stepped back into the room and into bed. Then she heard a number of low, dull thuds, like someone's fists striking on wood ... the sounds of someone reaching for a timber door. It was a groan, a groan, low and desperate. No animal would make such a sound. No ... they were human sounds, without a shadow of a doubt.

She climbed out of bed again. She just couldn't ignore it. Her upbringing had taught her that she couldn't ignore the sound of someone in pain, in suffering, not if she could help them in some way. Whoever was in trouble, it was only right and good that she gave them comfort.

Slowly, step by step, she left the room and made her way along the corridor. She would have to find the staircase to go downstairs, even if she could barely see her hands in front of her face, the darkness was so pitch-black. It was from somewhere on the lower floor that the sound was coming ... she followed it. Then, as suddenly as it had begun, everything fell silent once more. As silent as the grave.

Dorcas couldn't tell where was. She stopped. The corridor was deathly-cold beneath her bare feet, cold as ice. But, next thing, she heard it again. That strange moan – it came and went. It was best to keep going, although her common sense told her otherwise. She went down another set of stairs. Now she was close to the area that was off-limits to all of the castle's regular staff, the place that Cadi had warned her never to venture, no matter what the circumstances. And yet ... maybe this was her chance to see what was forbidden to her. There was a part of her that was still childlike and curious, a part of her that wanted to know ... and, after all, it was the middle of the night. Nobody would ever see her ...

She took the stairs that she'd never dared take before and followed the length of the forbidden corridor until she came to the giant pillars that formed the Main Hall. Moonlight streamed in through the high windows, just enough to help her make out the carvings within. She came to a stop as the magnificence of the sight struck her, even here in the dim light. The wondrous artwork, the riches of the imagination, where a number of giant arches intersected in the intricate patterns of a magnificent ceiling – everything was excess in this place, every inch so intricately carved! No wonder the servants such as herself were forbidden to wander these halls.

How many hours had such incredible artistry taken? The magic of the imagination in full flow. There was something otherworldly about it all ... this was far greater than any mortal hand could fashion. Even in her wildest dreams, little Mabli could never have have imagined anything as sumptuous and magnificent as this, the giant colums like great trees forming on all sides. Dorcas looked up at all the strange faces that appeared to stare down at her. She never had the time to study these so thoroughly during daylight hours. Each face was a unique and separate work of art – a sea of enormous eyes, a row of heads. One head had a giant tongue poking from it and huge teeth showing, another had two tongues emerging from either side of its great mouth!

Another, again, with its jaws exposed in threatening fashion ...

Suddenly, Dorcas felt a great fear engulf her. She'd ventured too far beyond her station, into the heart of the castle itself where she had no place ... It was as if the castle itself was a living, breathing thing, an entity that was watching her, rather than the other way around. For a moment, Dorcas felt an anger and shame engulf her. Why was she so afraid? Why was she so lacking in courage? Momentarily, she turned on her heels but then forced herself to retrace her steps and carry on. She was near the top floor of the castle now ... just one staircase away. But beyond the marble colonnade above, she saw something that made her blood run cold.

A pair of eyes stared at her – human eyes. She froze in her tracks and couldn't move.

What on earth was she going to do now? She didn't want to retrace her steps and return downstairs again. She had come this far, after all ... But then, she didn't know what trouble she might be in if she ventured further along the route that was forbidden to her. She stood stock-still for a moment, her feet frozen on the cold marble of that great staircase. Then, she got a second wind from somewhere and glanced upwards towards the top of that great building, as if sensing a presence. But no one was there – her imagination had run riot with all the stone faces and their enormous fiery tongues jutting out. Hestitantly, step by step, she reached the top of the great staircase.

Dorcas was rooted to the spot. A young man stood there in silence, watching her. He smiled.

"What a lovely surprise," he said as Dorcas lowered her eyes in embarrassment. The man was dressed in the finest of clothes and the smartest of shoes, and had the finest of English accents. She decided it was best to say nothing.

"So, what's a pretty lady like yourself doing wandering these corridors at this hour of the night?" the man said, moving closer to her.

"Sssorry, sir..."

The man came closer still, his eyes raised as if in a question.

"What's your name, lovely angel?" he asked encircling her waist with his arm and pulling her to him."Don't be scared, my love ..."

"My name is Dorcas, I'm a scullery maid here."

The man gave a quiet laugh.

"Are you now ... a scullery maid indeed!" He reached across and pulled her hair back from her face. "A very pretty scullery maid I might add ... particularly in this light."

Dorcas could smell the whisky on his breath.

"Please sir, you're scaring me," Dorcas said, sensing danger but the man pressed her in his arms.

"Shh ... no need to be scared my sweet angel. Just think of me as your friend. I like you, you beautiful little thing. What's your name?"

"Dorcas," she replied. "It's Welsh."

"Well now, Dorcas, my little Welsh angel. Are you lost, my dear?"

Dorcas nodded.

"No, don't you worry, you're not lost, my pretty one.

You've just come to a section of the castle that you're not supposed to visit ... But don't you worry, my love, I won't tell anyone. You won't be in any trouble. Oh no! You'll be fine. Where's your room?"

"Up ... on the top ... the top floor, off the third coridor," Dorcas stuttered, suddenly very frightened.

"Hold my hand, I'll show you the way back ... I'll be your guide."

The young man took her by the hand and led her further along the corridor. On reaching the third floor, Dorcas knew where she was again and she tried to pull her hand away.

"Thank you, sir, I'd best go now."

But the man paused, and gave her a strange and piercing glance.

"Go now, without so much as a thank you or any hint of gratitude? Surely not. I've taken quite a fancy to you now, my sweet one," he said, gripping her hand tightly. "Yes indeed."

"No sir. I best be off."

The man gave a strange smile.

"You want to leave?"

Dorcas nodded enthusiastically.

"I want to leave sir. Very much so."

"All right my sweet one. I'll have to let you go," he said, patting her on the arm. "Just one more thing ..." he whispered, placing his finger on her lips. "Just one kiss, my sweet angel ... is this too much to ask?"

Dorcas didn't understand much of what he said but she knew the meaning of 'kiss'. She didn't want to kiss him, and the English words came out strangely from her mouth.

"Very, very young, sir ... sorry."

This man's eyes twinkled in amusement at this.

"How old are you, Dorcas?"

"Fifteen."

"What a sweet and lovely age. What about one kiss? Just one small goodnight kiss?"

"No, sorry sir," Dorcas said, as the man leaned over and touched her breasts.

"Aren't you the sweet one, Dorcas ... what a lovely creature. Just one kiss and I'll let you go."

He pulled her to him and forced his lips on hers, even as Dorcas tried to fend him off with her arms.

"It's alright, my little Welsh angel. I'll just hold you tight a moment. I'll mind you in the darkness and take you up to your room."

Dorcas gave a shudder. She knew she was in grave danger. She tried to fight him off as he encircled her in an iron grip. She fought back against him but the Englishman was much stronger than her. He forced her onto the floor, and lifted her nightgown from her thighs.

"No!!!!"

He ripped her gown as she tried to twist away from him, but he forced himself on her and jammed her torn clothes into her mouth. Pushing her to the ground, he forced himself on her with all his weight.

"My lovely Welsh angel," he said, raping her over and over again as the pain tore through her, burning her very insides. And when his breathing slowed, he got up off her and walked away ...

Chapter 17

How long she had lain there, Dorcas couldn't tell. She took the torn material from her mouth. She was so thirsty. Her mouth was so dry, her lips were stuck to the roof of her mouth and she was dehydrated. She wept, then slept for a while, after which she woke up and shed more tears until she had no more tears left to weep, the cold floor pressing against her cheeks all the while. The corridor room was empty and dark and no one came near her through those long hours. She raised her head and peered downstairs. There wasn't a sound to be heard. Where had he disappeared? Did the monster plan to return to attack her again? Dorcas felt a terrible pain inside her body, like a great burning weight pressing down – it was as if the entire weight of the castle itself was towering over her. The only thing she could think of was getting back to her room ... somewhere where she could feel safe again.

Somehow, she raised herself from the ground and got to her knees as memories of the attack flooded her mind. She could scarcely believe it. She felt dazed, but the throbbing pain in her chest and thighs told her that it was all real ... it was all real ... the attack, her hopeless attempts to fend him off, the way she'd curled herself into a ball against him ... that monster ... she was like a frightened animal. How else had she ended up scrabbling around on her knees in this freezing corridor at midnight, her clothes half-torn?

She rose to her feet as a series of red-hot pains shot through her. She needed water. Slowly, she ventured her way along the corridors back to her room, pushing the door open. As soon as she got through the door, her body gave up and she fell down. The door swung back so quickly that it struck the wall, the noise loud enough to wake Cadi.

"Who's there?" Cadi shouted in a panic.

"Me, Cadi ... It's me – Dorcas."

Half asleep, Cadi reluctantly crawled out of bed, and lit a candle. "Dorcas! What on earth?!" she said as Dorcas collapsed onto the floor.

"Oh Dorcas, Dorcas, Dorcas ... Oh, no!!" Cadi cried as she saw her cousin's torn clothes. She lifted Dorcas's head from the floor and hugged her closely.

"Water, is it ..? There's no water here. Can you get up?" she said, trying to lift Dorcas onto the bed. "Here, try and ... Oh my God! My poor Dorcas, poor little Dorcas ... who did this to you? What animal ...?"

Cadi managed to lift Dorcas onto the bed where her poor cousin passed out almost immediately. All Cadi could do was sit by her bedside holding her hand until she came around again.

A few minutes later, Dorcas opened her eyes and realised where she was. "You need water, Dorcas ... But there's none here! I'm so sorry. We'd best wait for the call to get up, and I'll get you what you need, and help you wash yourself. You poor thing, Dorcas ... what happened? Tell me what happened, love. Did someone come in here when I was asleep and drag you outside?"

Dorcas explained how she'd heard the sound of crying, and why she'd left the room.

"There's a spirit in this house, an unhappy spirit. People hear it sometimes," Cadi said. "But you shouldn't have left the room; you should never leave the room, no matter what. I told you before, Dorcas ..."

Dorcas admitted to Cadi how she just couldn't have stayed in bed while listening to that terrible, pained cry. This was the first she'd heard of this unhappy spirit, this disturbed being that called out, then she told Cadi about the terrible thing that had happened to her, the rape. Cadi gave heavy sighs of despair. "I knew it," she said. "Oh my God, Dorcas! You poor thing. This is terrible ... these horrible monsters, these damned animals!"

Worse still, Cadi wasn't surprised that Dorcas had been so violently assaulted. "It's happened before, Dorcas, and it's still happening. It nearly goes with the job. This castle is that kind of a place ... there's something dark and sinister within these giant stone walls."

"Did the same thing happen to you, Cadi?"

"No, but I'm always terrified that it will. That's why I'm always so nervous and frightened all the time. You think I'm a bit too strict about the rules and regulations that go with the job ... but now you know why. I'm just so frightened all the time ... I'm deathly-scared, to tell you the truth."

A terrible realisation dawned on Dorcas. This had happened to other girls like her, there was nothing unusual in this ... it had happened before and would happen again.

"Life here's very dangerous when the gentry and their staff come to stay, Dorcas. I was trying to tell you to be on your guard, to warn you in my own way ... it's almost as if the guests feel that it's their right to assault the castle staff here ... that they're entitled to rape us ... It's like they own us, really, we're so far beneath them."

Dorcas described the man who'd raped her to Cadi, or what she remembered he looked like.

"He wasn't anyone on the lord's staff ... it was definitely one of his friends, I could tell by his clothes ..." she said, sobbing gently again.

"It doesn't make much difference to them, cousin. They're all the same. And we're all the same to them, too. We're just some of their fun while they're here on holiday ... it's like we're part of the hunt and the chase ..."

Cadi did her best but in that moment, her darkest hour, all Dorcas could think about was getting out of that prison of a castle, and getting home.

"I need to get away from here, Cadi. I need to escape ... I need Mam."

"That's only natural, being the first time ..."

"Could someone do this to me again, Cadi? Could one of these animals ... or the same one ... could they try and do it to me again? Oh God!"

"It's common enough, as I told you," said Cadi. "Anything can happen here. There's only one way of making sure, do you hear me? Never ... never, again – even if a dozen voices or spirits are calling to you – never, ever step outside your room at night. Don't even dream of it."

"And if I hear that tormented voice calling again, what should I do, Cadi?"

"Cover your ears and drown out the voices in your mind ... shout quietly over them. But promise me, on the pain of death, that you will not leave this room again at night ... ever! And the same goes if anyone tries to assault you again, day or night, start shouting at the top of your voice and keep shouting until help comes and your attacker runs away. Those animals will try and get their way with some other poor soul, you can be sure of that. It's a cruel place here ... it's everyone for themselves. You have to protect yourself as best you can."

Dorcas told Cadi that she'd tried to shout for help but that the man had put his hand over her mouth and shoved her to the ground.

"That was a vicious attack on you, Dorcas. And your clothes are all torn, the filthy brute ..." Now don't fall asleep, whatever you do ... it's almost time for us to get up for work."

"What am I going to do, Cadi? They can't expect me to get up in this condition. There's blood and I'm in terrible pain, it's clear as day for anyone to see that I'm badly hurt. I'm bleeding ... there's blood... I've been raped ... I'll have to stay in bed."

"That's not how the system works, I'm afraid. You have to get up and wash the same as every other morning and do a day's work, or Grantham will be down on you like a ton of bricks. I'll help you to wash yourself. Stay there for now – and I'll get you a drink of water as well."

Poor Dorcas had to get up in the end. How she managed to get through that day she'll never know. And, on top of that Miss Grantham, oblivious to what'd happened, had plenty of opportunities to scold her and find fault with her work. When they went to get clean caps and aprons to attend church later that morning, Dorcas stayed stretched out on the bed.

"I don't want to go to the service this morning, I can't, I just can't ..." she said, crying again, but Cadi gave her short thrift.

"You never want to go to the morning service, Dorcas, even at the best of times. This is your job now and this is what's keeping a roof over your head. Get up now quickly or they'll throw you out on the side of the road!"

When Dorcas didn't move and turned towards the wall, Cadi went over and shook her.

"Quickly, girl ..." she repeated urgently, putting on her apron and straightening her hair. "Get up now, Dorcas, put your apron on and follow me."

Dorcas sat up and glanced over at Cadi whose face was set in a determined grimace.

"You know, Dorcas, you're no different from any of the other girls who've been raped. You can't say a word to anyone ... come on quickly and we'll get ready to go to church. You're a maid, and you have no rights, it's as simple as that. That's your station in life and you're at the mercy of others for your food, your pay and your shelter. Come with me, quickly now ..."

The girls went downstairs and met the others who were standing quietly outside the door of chapel.

"You have to be last every day, you two, don't you?" said Miss Grantham, irritated.

"Sorry," Cadi replied immediately, responding for Dorcas as well, and both girls took their place at the back of the queue.

"In you lot go!" someone said, and they were prodded in through the doors with them. The moment Dorcas stepped through the door, she felt herself getting weak. They climbed a series of steps, Dorcas glancing at the tall columns overhead. To her, everything looked different now. All of the art had lost its wonder, and the chapel was no longer the same place anymore ... the world was no longer the same.

"It'll be fine, everything will be fine," Dorcas repeated, over and over to herself. A stone face stared at her from the top of one of the columns, as if coming alive. She turned away from it but felt it glare at her from the corner of her eye, its tongue hanging out. Suddenly, everything turned dark and Dorcas fell to the hard marble floor. The other maids and servants went on ahead but Miss Grantham stopped to see what was wrong.

"Stupid girl! Trust this silly one to cause a stir ... Go ahead! Everyone move!" Grantham barked in the direction of the others – everyone except Cadi.

"You take care of her, Cadi," Grantham ordered, "and make sure you sort her out," she said as she followed the others, the service about to begin. One of the servants had lingered for moment and she helped bring Dorcas to the kitchen to get a glass of water. They raised her into a sitting position and brought the water to her mouth. Gradually the poor girl came to.

"Don't go for a moment," Dorcas said to her cousin when she thought Cadi was about to leave to go about her tasks. "Please Cadi, I'm relying on you ..."

"Are you feeling better, Dorcas love?"

"Yes, thanks. I told you I didn't feel up to going in there. I was feeling so weak."

"Yes, but if you hadn't gone down to the chapel, Miss Grantham would have caused even more fuss. That's why I insisted that you go," Cadi said to Dorcas, whose face was as pale as death.

"In a flash, it all came back to me," Dorcas said, "right there when we went through the door of the chapel, it all came back as clear as day ... that awful thing ... I remembered it."

Cadi looked at her anxiously.

"Of course, it's still there ... it only happened a few hours ago, but whatever we do, we can't say anything to Miss Grantham about it!"

Dorcas looked up.

"Why can't we tell her? At least she'd understand then, wouldn't she?"

Sometimes, Cadi was amazed at how naive Dorcas could be.

"You won't get any sympathy from her, Dorcas."

"But he attacked me, for God's sake!"

"And he's perfectly entitled to do this, the way the gentry see it. As far as they're concerned, we're their property and we're just one of their many pleasures."

Dorcas threw her eyes up to heaven.

"I don't know what our parents would say if they knew what it was really like here. There's no way they'd ever have agreed to let us work here if they knew what might happen to us."

"But everyone accepts that this is the way the world works, Dorcas. I'm sorry, cousin."

The realisation that this was just another part of life was what disturbed Dorcas more than anything else. She'd been raped, and no one thought there was anything unusual about it. It was as if this was a normal part of a maid's life at Penrhyn Castle.

Chapter 18

Dorcas changed after the attack on her, there was no doubt about it. Some part of her was destroyed that night; something died in her. Maybe it was her self-respect, who knows? Dorcas herself couldn't say and she didn't spend time analysing it. It was a horrific way to discover that you were just dirt in the hierarchy of the castle, and that people had the right to do whatever they wanted with you. She listened to Cadi's advice and never left her room after midnight, even if she did hear the sound of that tormented spirit in the darkness ….

Hearing that anguished weeping come nightfall was a form of hell; she knew that the howl was a human one, even if she couldn't tell whether it was a man or a woman who was crying and weeping. She knew also that it was coming from within the castle walls, not from some desperate being wandering in the gardens outside. She learned to live with it. A tormented spirit wandered the corridors of the castle come midnight, and there was nothing she could do about it. Whatever it was, it never woke Cadi up, once darkness fell and her head touched the pillow. How many nights did Dorcas wake to that tormented voice, only to hear the regular rhythm of Cadi's breathing, heavy with sleep … Dorcas envied Cadi's powerful hold on sleep.

Whether real or not, Dorcas couldn't fail to empathise with this spirit. She suspected that it might be a girl of similar age to herself – a scullery maid, locked up and imprisoned somewhere deep within the bowels of that dark and sinister castle, an anguished and tortured being, begging for help. Whatever creature or spirit inhabited the castle, no one was listening to its torment, no one cared, and Dorcas knew exactly how this felt. This was the harsh truth of the new world she'd found herself in.

There was something else that disturbed her too. As the weeks passed, Dorcas had the strong sense that someone was watching her, even if it was never clear whether it was a creature made of spirit, or flesh and blood. She tried not to think too much about it, but when she came downstairs each morning, Dorcas was certain that this creature was watching her, even if she could never tell from where. It was the same while engaged in her daily work – she was aware of this presence – constant but invisible. On her way to the kitchens or passing along the corridors, she sensed a pair of eyes follow her every move, even if she never had any proof of it. She forced herself to ignore this presence, to learn to live with it, while praying that no one else would assault her again. The constant and ever-present fear of being attacked cast a deep shadow over her life, nonetheless. She was no longer the same cheerful or dreamy girl anymore. Her view of the world had darkened forever.

It was a permament change in her character, and there was no escape from this depression. Where once, Dorcas had woken up each morning looking forward to a new day, her life in Penrhyn Castle had changed all of that. The same never-ending drudgery of work and the constant worry of assault had destroyed her heart and her feel for life, and she felt older and more weary in herself. She no longer laughed or joked the way she once did. She found it difficult to find joy in her life, so much so that she often wore the same old dirty clothes from one day to the next. She didn't care how she looked and went for days without washing. If you spent your days cleaning up after others every day, what did it matter what you looked like yourself, especially if you were at the bottom of the heap? Lethargy became an integral part of her character.

The world of Tyddyn Pricia had disappeared completely; it was as if it had never existed or belonged to a country far away. Sometimes, it was hard to believe that there had been such a place. Dorcas felt that it had all belonged to a dream world she'd just imagined in her mind. It was as if she'd recreated the world of Long Ago – as inhabited by mythical and legendary characters who took the form of Ifan, Mabli, Lewis and Deio.

One person who noticed the change in Dorcas more quickly than most, and who was very worried about her, was Hanna. When Dorcas came to the castle initially she was like a breath of fresh air, and Hanna really loved her company. But now Dorcas was just a shell of her former self and she seemed to have lost interest in everything. There was a seriousness about her and she'd lost all interest and enthusiasm for the world around her. Not that Hanna blamed her. The castle was enough to overwhelm the happiest of souls.

"The gentry and all their minions won't be here forever," Hanna said to Dorcas one day as they spent hours in the kitchen washing and cleaning after a series of enormous meals.

"You're right, Hanna, even if I've nearly forgotten what that felt like – to have a normal day's work without all of these extra tasks to complete right into the dawn hours."

"Yes, our workload will be far smaller than it is now, and there'll be a lot less tension and stress around here, especially at meal times," Hanna reassured her.

"That'll be good," Dorcas said to her with a wan smile.

They completed setting the evening banquet for the lord's family and their entourage. Dorcas glanced momentarily at the table that had been set up for the gentry's feast, at the colours and the elegance of it all. An enormous trifle stood in the middle of the table, topped with a thick mountain of cream to form a spectacular display. There were giant walnuts, each one wrapped in specially fitted ribbons, and on two giant plates, one above the other, a magnificent selection of chocolates and fruits were laid out, all coated with sugar. The old Dorcas could have spent hours taking all of this in, enjoying the magnificence of the spectacle and display. But she wasn't the same girl anymore. She was someone else now, someone in whom all the beauty and happiness of the world had been destroyed. The sight of all this luxury and excess made her tired now. It disgusted her – the fact that everything was just a show. Part of her secretly hoped that someone might choke on all the stuff.

Hanna saw her looking.

"What do you think, Dorcas? Does it make your mouth water?"

"I've had enough of their sugary displays, never mind all the washing up we have to do afterwards," said Dorcas. "And as for trying to clean all that greasy syrup and the way they use so many pots and plates ..."

Sometimes, Dorcas wondered what things would have been like after the lord's departure. Then she realised that the one who'd raped her would have gone as well. This ought to have set her mind at rest, but she felt no peace at all. She'd never know who was the man who'd assaulted her. Worse again was the thought that whoever her attacker was, he would get away with it. He'd leave Penrhyn Castle unpunished, and his secret would go with him.

Dorcas would never get the chance to take revenge on him or get justice. She wanted revenge above all; she wanted to shout aloud against the injustice of it. She imagined him, the attacker, returning to his home in London, or wherever grand place he lived. Whoever he was, whether he was a member of the lord's family or one of his servants, she imagined him boasting and bragging to his pals about his conquest and the 'little Welsh angel' he'd taken advantage of. Dorcas clenched her fists tight in hate.

One day, while Dorcas was going around the table serving potatoes from a big china bowl to the senior servants from the lord's group, she noticed one person eyeing her with a sinister look. His eyes followed her around the room, and she hated the feeling of it – there was malice in them. Whoever he was – and she didn't recognise him at all – he had no right to stare at her the way he did. Dorcas went rigid and stiff with fear, and before she knew it the large dish had slipped from her fingers onto the ground and smashed into smithereens. Dorcas felt as if she was no longer in control of her own body, and as for the terrible silence that fell once the dish shattered on the floor … Everyone's heads turned to stare at her and a shocking stillness descended on the room. The man who'd been glaring at her all the while gave an arrogant smile in her direction. The other maids approached her to ask what'd happened and Miss Grantham was interrogating her before she knew it:

"Edwards, I might have guessed it was you. Can't you even keep a grip on a bowl of potatoes? For God's sake girl, what's wrong with you? On your knees, Edwards."

Dorcas looked at her.

"On - your - knees, I said. Now, girl …"

Dorcas had no choice but to obey. The other servant girls at the table thought it was hilarious and sniggered amongst themselves, nodding at her.

"Pick every piece up, and make sure the floor is clean and tidy. That was an expensive piece of china that you broke, and its price will be taken from your wages. You're not allowed to your dinner today either. You silly, silly girl!"

Sweeping up all the delicate pieces of china, Dorcas saw the image of the warrior's arm swinging the axe at the animal with the twin horns. It was as if she identified with the imaginary creature, waiting for the weapon to strike and fall.

Dorcas tried to hold back her tears until Miss Grantham had left, but try as she might, she failed to do so.

Chapter 19

The broken china bowl proved an ominous sign of what was to come, Dorcas would recall afterwards. And despite going a whole day without food, the experience proved worthwhile in another way. While the assault on her had changed her life, the broken bowl helped Dorcas restore her self-confidence in other ways. In a strange way, she realised that Miss Grantham and her minions couldn't control every single aspect of her life, and that it was possible to strike back against the system. And while breaking a dish was just something small in the greater scheme of things, the fact that she stood up to Miss Grantham showed that the castle and the assault there hadn't crushed her spirit completely.

Unsurprisingly, Cadi was worried at this new belligerence on Dorcas's part. Come evening, when they had a chance to chat, she warned Dorcas to watch her back again.

"Miss Grantham thinks you're starting to lose focus and that you aren't taking your duties seriously enough. "

"It was just a potato bowl, for God's sake!"

"But things like this don't happen if someone takes proper care. Did you smash that bowl deliberately?"

Dorcas glanced out through the window. Could she trust Cadi enough to share her feelings with her? She decided that it was better not to.

"No. Who would do something like that deliberately? The

bowl slipped, and I couldn't stop it crashing to floor. Accidents do happen."

"That's not how Miss Grantham sees things."

Dorcas stared at Cadi. Her cousin had a nervous, tormented look about her.

"Has she been questioning you about me?" she said accusingly.

Cadi gave an uncomfortable grimace.

"She's just trying to work out what happened with you … she's obviously worried about your mental state."

"Tell her not to worry about bowls and dishes is what I say," Dorcas responded defiantly, silencing Cadi. "If she was that worried about my condition, why did she starve me for the entire day?"

Cadi had no idea what was going through Dorcas's mind. One thing she was sure of was that her cousin was in grave danger of losing her job. As for Dorcas, she thought back on that incident when she'd smashed the bowl on the floor with nothing but pleasure. The sound of it smashing into a thousand pieces was a sweet memory to her, and it remained as clear as crystal in her mind, like a form of music. It was a sound she would have been quite happy to hear again and again. Unlike the sound of the crying and weeping she heard at night, there was nothing vague or sinister about it. It was the sound of Lord Penrhyn's property being smashed and destroyed into a thousand pieces.

It struck Dorcas suddenly, then, that she hadn't heard the sound of anyone singing for a long time. There had been a time, in her early days at the castle, when she'd sang songs herself regularly, espcecially in the mornings. The other servants had loved her singing and praised her for her fine voice. This seemed a very long time ago now. She knew that she'd never sing again inside the walls of that castle, no matter how much the others might have liked her to do so. At one time, before coming to Penrhyn Castle, singing had been such a large part of her world – singing at the church services, singing at the fair, singing at home, singing with the family, singing before going to sleep at night. So many lovely hymns, songs and ballads. And yet how rarely did anyone ever sing at Penrhyn Castle these day? Did the gentry ever sing on the other side of those thick walls that divided their part of the castle from everyone else? There was a pianoforte in there – she'd polished it countless times – and various other musical instruments that Dorcas and the others weren't familiar with. Maybe the gentry only sang when they'd had too much to drink – not that Dorcas had ever heard them.

Trapped there, in the confines in her room, many images and memories from her past came to Dorcas's mind. Some were very vivid, especially following her night-dreams, images that remained with her all day long. Other images disappeared again as quickly and would be gone before she woke up properly the next morning. Some of these thoughts were dark and filled with despair, and she did her best to force them from her mind again before they caught hold of her. So many thoughts and memories and so many hours to dwell on them – memories full of sights, sounds and smells.

Why didn't they give her some work to do while they kept her locked away in that room? It would have taken her mind off things and the time would have passed more quickly. Why didn't they give her a loom so that she could do something worthwhile? That used to be her skill, long ago. What she missed most of all was being out in the fresh air, the freedom of open air and sky. The window in the room was locked and the room smelled old and stale all the time. To Dorcas, who'd spent most of her youth outdoors in the fields, tending to the animals, or walking the country roads around the village, it was torment. Surely it was completely immoral what they'd done, holding her captive. Human beings were not supposed to be held in bondage like this. She was no better than a bird in a cage.

One day, she was cleaning one of the bedrooms by herself and the time was really dragging. She felt the urge to smash some more of the lord's property – the fighting spirit in her wanted to strike a blow against authority, to strike back against those who were keeping her down. She was cleaning the piss-pots, one of the dirtiest and lowest jobs of the lot, and she thought to herself that these too could be smashed into a thousand pieces. That would be funny now wouldn't it, she said to herself. Suppose they had no piss-pots at night! That would really annoy the crowd who thought they were so grand and posh now, wouldn't it?

How fragile were the pots? While washing one of them, she let it fall into the sink, and it cracked in two. Dorcas dropped the two pieces on the floor, and they crashed and broke into smithereens. She raised another piss-pot in her arms and let it fall. Crash! That joyful sound again. One after the other ... and then another again. She thought of stopping after five, but there was no point. She kept going until she had smashed more of them into pieces, until she had made her point. She knew that she'd be punished severely for this, so she might as well smash some more. But she didn't care by then. It didn't matter anymore.

She moved onto the last three bedrooms that needed cleaning and collected the pots from under the beds in them. She didn't even bother bringing them over to the sink for emptying and cleaning, but flung them straight onto the floor where they shattered loudly, the pieces of china flying in all directions! Next, she went into one of the rooms belonging to the gentry's personal servants. She wasn't supposed to touch their piss-pots but she checked to see if any of them had been emptied yet. No, they were still full! She tossed their contents over the beds, and smashed the pots against the wall.

Next thing, she heard the sound of footsteps running. There was no point in hiding. And anyway, she wanted them to see who'd made this huge mess. She went out into the corridor and saw two maids running towards her.

"Edwards! What's the matter? What's happening?"

They couldn't believe their eyes when they saw what she'd done.

"Just tell us, you dimwit ... who did this? Are you alright?"

The maids turned to one another in shock.

"There's nobody else here, Kathleen!"

"Has the culprit gone, Edwards? ... Are you alright, girl?"

A moment later it dawned on one of them.

"She did this, Kathleen, she did it herself. She's lost her mind completely! This girl is gone stone mad!"

Kathleen stared at Dorcas whose face was a picture of calm.

"Oh, good Lord, you're right! The Welsh goat is gone off her rocker ... Oh, Lawd ..."

Chapter 20

The hullabaloo that followed the smashing of the piss-pots was incredible. One would have thought that the Battle of Waterloo had begun all over again. Servants came running from all directions and grabbed hold of Dorcas, then dragged her to her room to await Miss Grantham's arrival. Miss Grantham had exploded with rage, of course. Dorcas would never forget her face – eyes white with rage and full of pure hatred. She ranted and raved so much that Dorcas decided it was safer to say nothing. There was no point.

"Why did you do this, Edwards? Why, Why? Why?" she spat at her, but Dorcas remained immune to her questions. The sole thought going through her mind was why she hadn't thought of smashing up the pots earlier. Why had she taken so long? The cost of the pots would be deducted from her salary, and she had to clean up the mess first. They left her there to clean up the room, remove the dirty bedclothes and bring them outside to wash them. Two other maids watched over her as she washed the bedclothes and other items. She swept up all the broken china and returned to the room to normality. By then, Miss Grantham had decided on a more severe punishment for her.

And this was how she'd found herself confined in this empty, furnitureless room at the back of the castle, with one tall window high up, and just a blanket and the hard floor to sleep on. She'd been there for days now, and the only contact she'd had with the outside was when someone called by with food three times a day. There was no toilet in the room, just a bucket in the corner that she emptied herself each morning. Also, she was handed a bowl of water and a linen to wash herself every morning, but her ablutions were supervised and there was one of the maids watching her.

"For the moment, we're not supposed to let you wash yourself unsupervised," the maid had explained one morning. "You might smash the bowl."

"I don't care," said Dorcas. She was used to the presence of other women by then.

"Why did you do it?" asked the other maid. "That's what we want to know."

Dorcas ignored her.

"You're a strange one, aren't you? Making a right scene like that! My God! And everyone's talking about you since then ... all the staff. They think you've lost your mind completely, and that you've gone completely crazy! But I don't think you are, are you?"

"I don't care," said Dorcas, leaving the cloth by in the water bowl.

"Isn't it awfully lonely here on your own?" the maid said, trying to get Dorcas to open up.

"I don't care," Dorcas repeated, and this was was the only answer they could get out of her.

The days and nights passed, one melting into the next. One of the few benefits of being locked away like that was not being forced to attend the daily church service. Maybe, subconsciously, that had been her objective. By now, there was no contact between her part of the castle that housed the workers and the staff, and the living quarters where the lord and his family lived. Without having to perform the serving duties daily, she could try and block off and forget her great fear of the other side of the castle. It didn't stop this image from haunting her mind and her every waking moment, however. The memory of what'd happened that terrible night was as alive in her mind as if it'd only happened yesterday. She could see his hungry eyes and feel his dirty fingers, and then it was as if the stone faces on the columns came alive and were laughing at her predicament all over again. She couldn't keep those horrible images away.

Worse still, what would her parents say if they knew their daughter was being held prisoner? What would the people of Dolgellau say? They would be shocked that she, Dorcas, was being treated in this way. Perhaps she had misbehaved, but to be punished like this was extreme and went beyond all reason. Any normal prisoner would have been told the length of their sentence, but poor Dorcas had no idea how long she would be kept locked up in that dingy room. She wasn't even sure what part of the castle her room was in.

One day, she did hear a bird singing clearly somewhere outdoors and so she knew she must be somewhere near the castle walls. The sound of the birdsong gave her great comfort and a sense of calm for a while. Listening to that small bird's voice, so wild and free – Dorcas knew that this awful time would eventually pass. She would be able to look out through the windows again one day at the birds of the air and the animals of the fields, and she would be free again to go outdoors once more. This trouble would surely come to an end ... as long as that bird continued singing.

But one sound remained ever-present and unchanged to her ears, and these were the moans and cries of those poor souls who suffered in the darkness of night. Was it the sound of the castle's tormented spirit weeping? If she were to believe what Cadi said, this was the noise and commotion she heard come nightfall. Dorcas woke up often to hear it – the quiet sobbing and then the loud crying and howling noises like thunder. It pained her to hear them – these horrible cries that were now part of her every night in that castle. And the worst thing of all was the fact that she was helpless to save those poor suffering creatures or help them in any way.

One night, on hearing those familiar cries, Dorcas got up off the ground and went to the door to see how close the sobbing and tears were. No, the noise still seemed quite far away.

"Who is it?" she heard herself say. "Why are you crying?"

The sound suddenly ceased.

"Hello, I'm Dorcas ... I'm a prisoner here ... please tell me who you are – who's there?"

The noise sounded again. Maybe she was slightly mad to be talking to a ghost or spirit like this. But what if it wasn't a ghost? Who wouldn't respond to the creature that emitted this sound, the world's saddest cry?

Whoever or whatever it was, it didn't want to talk to her, and Dorcas lay back down on the hard ground again. Next, she awoke to a louder voice – or was it a series of voices? At first, she heard them chanting. It sounded like dozens of people together. Dorcas sat up at the sound. Then the voices fell silent again and there was the sound of weeping and sighing, and the gnashing of teeth. Then more roaring and screaming before Dorcas realised what these tortured sounds were – these were the voices of hell calling to her. She was to be brutally punished for her behaviour, and these sounds were a prelude to what lay before her. She'd been a very wicked girl and now she'd have to pay for her sins.

These voices and anguished moans and cries disappeared again come bright morning. Each new day, Dorcas would trace the paths of her childhood in an effort to recall happier times. Little scenes came to mind, glimpses of home that had stayed with her. Rhys looking up at her expectantly on the day of the fair, Lewis walking with her through Cae Isaf, Ifan guiding her arm on the loom, her mother's gentle touch before sleep. She thought of the animals she'd loved so well back home and her work with them – guiding Neli the cow from Cae Uchaf, collecting the eggs from the chickens, Lewis playing with the suckling lamb. She tried to recall the faces of her friends and bring them to mind again, the way they'd always been joking and laughing together. She filed away all her fondest memories and the warmth of friends and home. It seemed so long ago since she'd been combing Lisa's hair and arranging the daisies in her long tresses ... What would she not give now to be back home in Tyddyn Pricia again, and her mother making her a plate of lunch. It was hard to believe that this other world still existed somewhere out there ...

Dorcas heard a key rattle in the door and a voice saying

her name. It had been a long time since she'd heard her name pronounced the Welsh way.

"Hey, Dorcas, are you there?"

It was Hanna! She recognised her voice immediately!

The door opened and there was Hanna, standing there, a bowl of porridge in hand.

"Hanna! It's you!" Dorcas rushed to her and hugged her.

"Dorcas …" Hanna said nodding ruefully. "Dorcas, sweet Dorcas!"

Oh how good it was to hear a kind voice at last! Dorcas began to weep. She hadn't felt another human being's touch for so long. Hanna looked at her compassionately.

"Oh little Dorcas, look at you! You're a right scary sight, aren't you … Don't cry, please. "

Dorcas looked at her friend.

"I haven't cried until now. Everyone has been horrible to me, just giving me abuse constantly, and look – I see someone kind for the first time in ages and I'm heartbroken and crying."

Hanna sank to her hunkers.

"Here, look, I've brought you a little bite to eat, it's nothing great, but it's all they'd give me …" Hanna said, producing a piece of bread from beneath the folds of her apron.

Dorcas crouched down and ate quickly. Now that she tasted food, she realised how ravenous she was with hunger.

"How on earth did you manage to bring this into me?" she said between mouthfuls.

"Alison was supposed to bring it into you but I said that

I'd make all the dinners and suppers today if she let me in to see you. I was nearly going mad worrying about you."

Dorcas gave a groan and began to cry again.

"But here's what I have for you," Hanna said, reaching into her beady pocket. "Something sweet for you."

It was an apple. Dorcas eyes widened with delight.

"Thank you, Hanna," she said, weeping gently again. Hanna put her arm around her shoulders.

"It's disgraceful that they're punishing you in this way."

"Has anyone said anything about when they're going to let me out of here?"

Hanna bit her lip.

"There's been no word yet. Fair play to your Cadi, though, she's asked Miss Grantham more than once ..."

Dorcas raised her eyes in hope.

"And what did she say?"

"She told Cadi that it's none of her business. She says that you deserve to be punished severely for what you did."

"Ada said that the others were all talking about me ..."

"That's true. The rumour is that you've gone crazy, that you're stone mad."

"Oh, no ... Now they'll treat me like I'm some kind of a wild animal when they finally release me from here."

"It's good to see you, Dorcas. I've been so worried about you."

"Can you tell which part of the castle I'm in?"

"You're in that small basement room closest to the cellars. Don't you feel how much colder it is down here? And it smells awful here as well."

"I must be so used to the smell by now, I've been here so long. What's it like outside today?"

"It's a little bit sunny, and it's windy outside too ..." said Hanna, unsure as to why Dorcas was asking.

"There's no window here, apart from that small one high up there, so I can't tell what things are like outside."

Dorcas finished eating the porridge and Hanna looked across at her.

"You don't even have a mattress ... are you sleeping alright?"

"I hear voices at night ..."

"What kind of voices?"

"Voices of people suffering and in pain. The sound of someone crying and weeping as if their heart is broken, and then this terrible tormented moaning ... Cadi says that she's heard that there's some kind of a ghost or spirit in here. Have you seen this spirit or heard it?"

Hanna gave her an anxious look.

"Have you?" Dorcas asked.

"Yes, and they say it's not a spirit that belongs to Penrhyn Castle ... but something that comes from somewhere else ..."

"What's that, Hanna?"

"I've heard rumours that these awful sounds are the spirits of slaves."

"Here? But there aren't any slaves here ..."

"The lord has hundreds of slaves, they say. Do you remember the pictures on the wall in the dining room, the pictures that showed the black people in them?"

"The pictures of Jamaica and the West Indies, weren't

they? But the people in those pictures looked like they were happy, that they had a pleasant life working out on the fields."

Hanna shook her head.

"I've heard rumours that they're being treated terribly over in those countries. They say that they're treated worse than animals over there," says Hanna with an anguished look.

"I remember a man who came and spoke to us at the fair in Dolgellau once saying that the truth was that the slaves in the West Indies were regularly beaten and abused ... that they're kicked and whipped ... and worse things again ..." Dorcas said, falling quiet.

"Well, I've only heard the stories about this ... the rumours ..." Hanna went on, "and there are many people who don't want to believe these stories either ..."

Hanna and Dorcas looked at one another.

"But what if these stories are really true?" Hanna asked, breaking the silence while looking into her friend's eyes.

"That's why I'm so frightened hearing these voices," says Dorcas. "They're so real ... I hate to think of them, even – their awful suffering. At first, I thought these were voices from hell ..."

"It's the hell of the slaves that you're hearing once night falls. The more I hear about these spirits haunting this castle, I'm sure of it now. These are the tormented spirits that you and others are hearing."

Hanna couldn't stay long. She stood up to leave.

"I really hope they let you out soon Dorcas, my friend."

"Thank you, Hanna. Thank you so much. Goodbye."

Dorcas went over what Hanna had said afterwards. And she compared it with the speech that the man at the market in Dolgellau had made too. One thing he'd said that day still stood out clearly in her mind: "The only difference between us and them is the colour of their skin, but this is no reason for others to treat these people as animals!"

That night, Dorcas had great difficulty falling asleep. The sounds of human beings suffering and their tormented wailing was worse than before, far worse. Now that she understood its source, she felt more frightened than she had ever been.

Chapter 21

How long did they want to keep her there? And for what purpose? Dorcas couldn't tell. She asked to speak to Miss Grantham a number of times but nothing ever came of it. Maybe they planned on dimissing her once she'd completed her punishment, Dorcas thought. And secretly, she hoped that this was what they would decide – the thought of being free again and getting away from that castle was the only thing that kept her sane. The thought of that big sturdy door being unlocked, and being free once more! If she had to walk all the way to Dolgellau in her bare feet, so be it. It would have made no difference to her. Each step would bring her closer to the heaven that was Tyddyn Pricia again.

There had been a time when Dorcas was very anxious about losing her wages, and the difficulties this would cause for her family back home, but she didn't care anymore. And as soon as she knew what'd happened to her there, her mother would forgive her immediately. Getting away from Penrhyn Castle – this was the only thing that mattered to Dorcas now. Escaping the clutches of this horrible family, the devil in the form of Miss Grantham, and all the false grandeur of the place. Escaping home where she'd be back in the embrace of her family again – back to her family and the people of Dolgellau. Back to the old routine where she could speak Welsh every day, go to the chapel, visit her friends – and sing and dance – and just live again!

Later that morning, Ada came to unlock the door, but she didn't have the water bowl with her this time. She brought in a bowl of porridge instead and placed it on the floor and stood there without a word while Dorcas ate it.

"Am I not being allowed to wash this morning?" asked Dorcas once she'd eaten.

"Miss Grantham says that you are to have a bath today instead," Ada said, finally opening her mouth.

Dorcas was surprised at this.

"A bath! That's a real luxury! It's been weeks since I've been allowed to have a bath. How come she wants me to have a bath now?"

"I don't know," says Ada, with a blank look. "Are you finished?" she says impatiently, taking the empty bowl from Dorcas. "Someone will be back to you later." Ada locked the door again behind her and quickly left.

Having a bath would give Dorcas a chance to wash her hair, and this would prove a blessing. For days, her scalp had been so itchy and greasy that it had become a form of suffering. To be able to wash her hair would be pure bliss, as would having her entire body washed clean in water. There would almost certainly be someone there keeping a close eye on her, but she would just ignore them and try and escape into her own little world.

But the big question was why? Why the bath today? Why was today an exception? Her great fear was that her period might begin today – she had lost count of the days of the month. That would be terrible if Miss Grantham refused to let her have some period cloths. So far, she'd been lucky in this one regard. In her subconscious, she wished for her period to come, but she wouldn't allow herself to consider the other possibility. She said a quick prayer that this wouldn't happen. It was too frightening to think about and she forced this thought from her mind.

Why? Why now for the bath? This was what really worried Dorcas. Was it Hanna who'd succeeded in arranging this for her? This was unlikely, if Miss Grantham had had anything to do with it. It struck Dorcas, then, that this might be a prelude to her leaving the castle ... Maybe, they were throwing her out and maybe she'd lost her job! This bath might have been the preparation for her departure! Home, returning home ... that was the only thing on her mind now. When the door was next unlocked, there was no signg of Hanna or Ada either. This time it was Alison who was stood in the doorway.

"Your bath is ready," she says, spitefully and doing a mock-curtsy. "Why are you getting a bath anyway, considering what you did? This is all I want to know. Who 'ave you bribed? Cor, I started to fill it, and it took me 'alf an hour. Who's 'aving the bath I asks, and they says 'Edwards' ... Cor, it doesn't 'alf stink in 'ere. 'Aven't you emptied that bucket yet?"

Dorcas gave her a look of contempt.

"I can't empty it if they don't open the door, can I?"

"Well, empty it now before you 'ave your bath. There's no point 'aving a bath and then coming back to a stench like this, is there? The other maid should 'ave reminded you, girl."

Dorcas walked to the back and picked up the bucket that needed emptying. At least it was only her own dirt that she had to dispose of. It was a lot better than having to empty twenty piss-pots belonging to others. Dorcas wondered if they had new piss-pots now that she'd destroyed the others. Alison was still standing at the door.

"Ready? Follow me now."

They went upstairs and down to the end of the corridor. Dorcas was surprised to see Miss Grantham there waiting for her, a set of clothes in her arms.

"I'm supervising your bath, Edwards, and then you put these on."

Dorcas looked her in the eyes. Miss Grantham had a grim and determined look about her, a hateful look, truth be told. Dorcas kept quiet.

"You understand what I'm telling you now, Edwards? Or are you still the same mute Welsh goat that you were before? You may leave us now, Alison ... Come back in quarter of an hour to empty out the bath-water."

Alison gave a grimace of disgust.

"But shouldn't she empty 'er own water?" she asked. "I'll be damned if I have to wait around for this one to finish!"

"Excuse me, Alison, but have you forgotten who you're talking to here?" Grantham growled. "Do as I say, or you'll be severely punished too!"

Alison left.

Having to strip while Miss Grantham looked on immediately destroyed any pleasure Dorcas might have taken from the bath. It was a duty now, a duty filled with judgement and shame. She climbed into the water. It was lukewarm, a small sliver of soap floating on the top. She felt embarrassed and ashamed doing everything while Miss Grantham looked on. Meanwhile, Grantham just stood there without uttering a word. There was no sense to it. A few short minutes later and the older woman says:

"Time is up. Get out now."

Silently, Dorcas did what she was told and went over to the chair where Miss Grantham had left the clothes. They were much better than her normal clothes. Why was she getting smart clothes? Was it a case that the Penrhyn crowd were so high-and-mighty that they'd only let their maids leave the castle wearing fine clothes? Dorcas was confused.

"Am I being sent home? Am I being removed from service here?"

She never forgot the look Miss Grantham gave her at this, a stare of complete bewilderment.

"Home?"

"You don't want me to work here anymore?"

Miss Grantham stared at her for a long time.

"No. You're still employed here, Edwards. We don't pay mountain goats like you to make a mess like you did in Penrhyn. But we're not going to let get you away with it that easily. You're going to be in service here for another while ... We're not going to put you in the kitchen anymore, probably, considering you're so much of a liability."

"Miss Grantham, I can't work for you anymore. Aren't I allowed to leave? Isn't it my right to go home if I want to?"

Miss Grantham laughed at this.

"You have rights now, do you? After the way you behaved? Don't make me laugh, will you? You have no rights, and you're going to have to pay back every penny you owe for the damage you did recently. Every single penny! I'm going to make life hell for you, Edwards! There's no way we're going to let this go."

A terrible sense of dread ran through Dorcas. She felt like she was going to vomit. So they weren't going to let her go? She was trapped in this awful castle for the forseeable future, whether she liked it or not.

"Follow me," Miss Grantham ordered Dorcas.

And as a lamb to the slaughter, Dorcas walked behind Miss Grantham upstairs, past the nasty looks directed at her by many of the other servants. Immediately, Dorcas felt on trial. The dirty looks of the others were part of the of the ominous and oppressive atmosphere of the castle from now. They climbed a series of steps and went around the gallery to a door at the end of another corridor that Dorcas had never seen opened before. Miss Grantham rapped on the door, and a man's voice answered from within. Miss Grantham turned to Dorcas and gave her a look of deep contempt.

"You're no good to me for the moment but here's someone that you might be of some use to, perhaps," she said, pushing the door open.

Dorcas stood stock-still and found herself facing her greatest nightmare. There he sat at the dinner table without a care in the world – the man she'd never wanted to lay eyes on again.

"My lovely Welsh angel," he said in his cold voice. "You've returned."

Chapter 22

Dorcas heard the door shut behind her and it was like the sound of a coffin-lid being slammed closed forever. She felt dizzy and short of breath and was rooted to the ground with horror. She just couldn't believe it. She had prayed she would never lay eyes on him again, and yet here he was, just inches away from her – that creature – the monster who'd attacked her. Here he was casually eating what was left of his lunch. She watched him swallow the last few mouthfuls of meat on his plate, the gravy dribbling from his lips. He unfolded his napkin and wiped his mouth clean before speaking.

"Delightful ... what a lovely surprise. I wondered what was for dessert today and now you you've appeared! How wonderful is that?" he said, with a twisted smile. "Why are you looking so frightened, my dear? Such a sweet and innocent girl! Come here to me ..."

Dorcas hesistated. She was petrified and unsure of what to do. She didn't want to go anywhere near him and she'd have to play this game carefully. On the other side of the room stood a luxurious bed and a bedspread decorated with red velvet and golden roses. Why was this creature eating his meal in his bedroom?

"Come here and sit on my lap, my sweet," he purred.

What was his 'lap'? She didn't understand what he meant. There was a stool near the dining table and Dorcas sat down on it facing the man.

"You'd rather sit there? Fine by me, my dear. Have you had your dinner today? I haven't anything left, I'm afraid ... It was lamb today ... Tasty Welsh lamb, fine and succulent with potatoes and peas. Do you do any of the cooking in the castle? Answer me when I speak to you ... What's your name again?"

"Dorcas."

"Yes ... and you're Welsh, aren't you, Dorcas?"

Hearing her name – Dorcas – on his lips digusted her. She wanted him to spit the word out again and give back to her what was hers.

Dorcas glanced at the table. The best of china laid out, coloured red and gold. She noticed the Penrhyn coat of arms, with the arm and the hammer. She stared at the wine glass, the coffee cup, the sugar bowl, and the solid-silver spoons. She glanced at the dirty knife and fork – the same utensils that she polished in the kitchen each day until they sparkled.

"You look so sad, Dorcas ... what can I give you? Would you like some wine?"

Dorcas shook her head, avoiding his eyes.

"Let me drink my coffee before it gets cold. Look, would you like a sugar cube ... Here, take one, Dorcas, won't you?"

The creature leaned over to her, the sugar lump in his hand but Dorcas turned away in the direction of the door. How in the world was she going to escape his clutches? There was no way out.

"Open your mouth, girl."

Dorcas stared at him with all the hatred she could muster. What right did he have to order her around?

"Here. Open that lovely little mouth of yours when I tell you," he said more threateningly this time.

Dorcas took the sugar lump and put it in her mouth.

"There you are, isn't that sweet? Do you like it?"

There was no escaping him.

"Have you lost your tongue, girl?" he asked, rising from his chair, annoyed.

"No, sir."

More gently this time, he placed his hand on her shoulder.

"There's no need to 'sir' me ..."

He pulled her closer and caressed her throat and neck with his lips. Dorcas blushed.

"You're still shy, aren't you little one? Didn't you enjoy our last encounter?" His fingers traced the length of her face and neck and paused above her collar.

"No sir," said Dorcas as firmly as she could, and raised her hand to stop him.

"No need to be coy with me," he said, kissing her finger.

Dorcas felt as if she was trapped in a spider's web. Her heart was pounding and she was breathless with fear.

"Or is this how you drive men crazy? Look at me, girl."

His finger beneath her chin, he pushed her face upwards so that his eyes met hers. "What is it, Dorcas? How can I make you happy?"

"I want to go. I want to get out of here!"

"But you've been a naughty girl, haven't you? That's what I've heard ..." he said, his stubby finger still fixed beneath her chin. "You've been locked up and kept prisoner, all on your own girl, haven't you?"

Someone had told him everything that had happened.

"And I didn't like the idea of my little Welsh angel all on her own, so I said to them 'Let her go, let Dorcas go'. And they did ... Because I'm your friend now. I'm here to protect you, isn't that so?"

"Then let me go. If you're really my friend, won't you let me go? Can't you see that I'm very frightened here?" She stared into his eyes and begged. "Please let me go ... Please sir." Was there any point in reasoning with him?

He gave her a sad look and shook his head.

"I can't, Dorcas. They'll lock you up again. Stay and keep me company for a while. Let's have some fun. Come here and sit on my knee, girl ..."

He sat on the chair forcing Dorcas to sit on his lap. He began to stroke her back with his hand. "Let me have some more wine first."

Dorcas watched him reach for the bottle and swallow back another great swig of wine. The creature was at home, in his own lair and in complete control of the situation. There was no escaping him – not a chance.

He turned his face to hers. "Kiss me, Dorcas," he whispered and stroked her hair.

The man was half-drunk. His stale-wine tongue forced her lips open and dug deeper into her mouth and Dorcas wanted to vomit. His arms circled her and he squeezed her tight and tighter still, then pulled her downwards until they slid off the chair onto the floor. The man pushed himself against her, his hands wandering beneath her clothes again as he surfed his own wave of pleasure.

Dorcas reached for the knife on the plate that was above their heads and took hold of it, unknown to him. He continued to push himself against her, holding her in an iron grip, but she managed to bring the meat-knife down with great force from behind his head, planting it deep in the man's neck. Blood splurted from him, pumping from his throat and with a great choking sound, his head fell sideways and struck the floor.

Dorcas, who was still trapped beneath him, tried to wriggle herself free, but she struggled with the enormous weight of him. The creature's body gave a few vicious jerks as the blood sprayed from his mouth and throat but then he fell still as the life went out of him. She couldn't have?! Yes, there was no doubt about it ... he had taken his last breath.

Dorcas pulled herself out from beneath him and struggled to her feet, then stared transfixed at the creature's limp body on the floor. What in the world had she done? Her blood was pounding and she couldn't breathe anymore. Had she really ...?

Yes. His eyes were dead and he was gone. The monster was no longer free to threaten all and sundry. He could attack and rape no more – neither her nor any other poor unsuspecting girl. They were free of him forever ...

Her delight was short lived. She might have put a stop to this monster but if she was in trouble before, she was in a much greater bind now. There was no point in making a run for it ... they would only catch her immediately and lock her up again – forever maybe, this time ... And there was no point in saying that it was an accident either – they'd probably just mete out the same treatment to her in revenge. As the severity of her situation dawned on her, Dorcas did the only thing possible.

She rushed to the window, opened it and jumped.

And this is the last we hear about Dorcas.

We don't know what happened to her afterwards. She disappeared and there's no record of what happened to her from then on.

Her story ends
        as she finds herself
                caught between
                        two worlds

and all we can do is to guess at her likely fate.

    Did she survive the fall from the window
                or was she mortally injured?
                        Does it matter in the end?

She was just an ordinary maid, an ordinary woman who lived at a particular time in history. Whether she survived her escape attempt or was re-captured, her fate may have proved much the same. She is lost. The parish records for that time include no reference to a Dorcas Edwards. There's no history of her sudden death, no record of an inquest. Whether she survived her escape and had a new life after this, we will never know. There's no trace of her in the official documents or the history books because such books demonstrated little or no interest in the lives of the ordinary people – or a lowly maid or servant such as Dorcas.

If she did survive, however, Dorcas would no doubt have found the following diary of great interest ...

EBONY'S STORY

Running, running like the wind, her legs fast and strong, running to God knows where, slower then faster again, her body leaning forward into the wind, feeling the freedom. Who cares where? Just running as far away as possible, escaping that crazy hell.

Run, Ebony, run ... she's fleeing in terror but she doesn't care anymore ... her body could break into a thousand pieces and be scattered to the four winds.

She doesn't care anymore because she's lost everything now ... everything's gone. Any small hints of happiness slipped through her fingers long ago. They've long since disappeared.

Barefoot, her graceful fifteen-year-old body moves to a rhythm all of its own, across the plantation fields, her soles striking stones and hard ground. She feels the blood pumping through her, coursing through her, body and soul. The stink of smoke on the air makes breathing difficult. But there's nothing else. Run, Ebony, run for your life. Just the traces of your feet left behind on the rough dry soil. Traces that soon disappear ... traces of her passing.

As with her memory of what came before, this too is the best thing that can happen, because the less Ebony remembers of her young life, the better by far ...

A DIARY THAT ISN'T A DIARY

This will not be a real diary. I can't write. In truth, this is nothing like a diary. This is a record of my thoughts and feelings, and if I had paper or ink, and if I could write, maybe it would sound something like this ...
But I have no materials to write with and no page on which to convey the words.

This record here may be nothing more than a bit of company, a whisper in the ear of a friend. Maybe this is what I crave foremost of all here – a friend the same age as me, someone I could share my hopes and fears with. I can divide my life into three parts – the beginning, my life with Hagar, and my life after Hagar was gone. I may be only fifteen years old but I feel like I've already lived my life three times over. I hope there's a life after this one. When this time comes – as it did for Hagar – and I'm certain that they, the slavemasters, will prevail in the end, I like to think there's another world waiting for us after this one, and that one day I can look back on this life and thank God that I managed to survive.

IN THE FIELDS

We were out in the fields cutting cane again, and the heat was brutal. I think we can survive the heat if we aren't physically abused too much. But seeing other workers here being abused daily is a torment and very difficult to cope with. Watching Sancho being whipped this morning in our presence, for doing nothing, disturbed all of us. At first we put our heads down and pretended nothing was happening. And the Vulture must have noticed, because he snarled and flogged Sancho even more viciously than before. Because we were afraid, none of us shouted out in protest or challenged the Vulture. We just stared at him with cold hatred instead because the next moment he was roaring between each stroke of the whip:

"What are you lot looking at? On with your work, you pigs!"

No one moved. It was as if we were rooted to the ground, standing still and staring ... What else could we do? The Vulture pulled back from us momentarily, as if feeling our hatred on his skin. There was no let-up in his whipping of Sancho, however, not until he'd left him bloodied and unconscious on the ground.

"That's enough," blurted out Roger, the eldest person among us.

"That's enough."

"What did you say?" said the Vulture, shocked that someone had dared to speak.

"Enough," we all said in unison.

The Vulture turned to Roger.

"Enough ... enough ... enough," everyone murmured as one, in a low chant.

Roger bravely stared into the Vulture's face head-on but suddenly he too felt the lash of the whip. The Vulture exploded in anger and lashed him across the back and the face, and then across the legs until Roger fell to the ground. The chanting fell quiet and the Vulture looked at us menacingly.

"I'm the only one who's allowed say 'Enough' around here, understood?" and walked away.

No one uttered a word. Once he was out of sight, we lifted Roger off the ground and the men dragged poor Sancho's limp and unconscious body away.

ONE ENDLESS STRING OF TIME

The White Man divides his time into months and years, each of which he can number and record. He likes to divide time up and enumerate things. I can't understand his ways myself.

Having divided the year into different pieces of time, he does the same with each day that passes. Every portion of every day has a number, and he owns a machine in his pocket which he uses to identify time and divide it up. This is very strange. Maybe it stems from the idea that he owns time, that he possesses it like so many other worldly materials. Whenever he doesn't have a period of time portioned out, or doesn't need to share his time with others, he's a man of leisure and free to do what he wants. The time-measuring machine would look nice in my pocket (if I had pockets, or if I had any valuables to store in them!). But if you do the same thing every hour of the day, and every day and week of the year, what do you need days and weeks for? What do years mean? Time is just one long and endless string, one that stretches on infinitely with neither beginning nor end.

IN THE LAND OF MEMORIES

Another thing the White Man does is map places. He makes a picture of the lands he owns and marks them with shapes and squares on large pieces of paper. And he thinks that he controls this land and that it's his forever, that it's a part of him. He's obsessed with material things, their ownership and control. If someone was to ask what's the greatest fault of the White Man – and there are plenty of them – I'd say it's the way he tries to possess everything. Our lands, our clothes, our time, our money, our housing, our livestock, our people – the White Man must own them all. "It's mine" is his constant refrain, like the child in the cradle.

The biggest flaw in this way of thinking is that there's never enough land for him to possess, there are never enough goods or wealth; he always wants more. This endless craving for more is like a dog pissing on his patch to show that he owns it. He wants more just to have more, but also to show his friends that he has more than they have. It means so little in the greater scheme of things, but the phrases "I love this" and "it's mine" is the basis of his life.

It was all so different in the Land of Memories. Back there, it was our community who owned the land, and only temporarily. Each generation lived and died but the land always remained, as did the good that it produced for our benefit. The land existed before we were born, and it would be there long after we left. The land is permanent whereas we, the people, are always passing through. In the meantime, it's our responsibility to cultivate and protect the land.

Back in the home country – in the Land of Memories – if anyone of us had stood up and announced that a section of land was "their land" we would have laughed at them and reminded them of the truth. What mortal being can own land? It's not something you can put on a donkey and cart and take it away. The land gives to us, it nourishes us and gives us food so that we can live, so Grandpa would always say back in the Land of Memories. And when our time in this world is over, what remains of us returns to the land, to the earth once more. What is the earth and the land but the guardian and the spirit of our ancestors?

Strange, too, how I remember Grandpa's words so many years on and so far away from our home in the Land of Memories. I still remember the smell of his skin even after all this time, his wrinkled face and the distant look in his eyes. The memories are as living things. I remember following the stone path to the fire, and settling down on the ground amongst the women to listen to the familiar myths. I miss those feelings more than anything, that feeling of firm ground beneath me, the feeling of safety and belonging that was once ours and which I haven't felt for so long.

I never imagined then that these feelings of security and love could ever come to such an abrupt end. When I stared up at the stars as a child and gave them their names, I never imagined for a moment that my childhood world would come tumbling down and the stars crash and fall to Earth, smashing into pieces. Are they still up there high above, our childhood stars that twinkled bright, I wonder, or have they crashed to Earth, the same as Hagar and I? Do the stars too feel lost and alone, as we do? Do they remember us? Is their light still trying to find us?

The big difference in the Land of Memories was the love that bound us all tight and kept us all strong. Not just father and mother, but the love of Grandpa and Nague and everyone in the village. We were all one family, we were all the same tribe. Here in this foreign land, we've been brought in chains. No one is related, there are no bonds between people except the bonds of slavery; everyone's from a different place, everyone's from somewhere else. All we can say for certain is that there are Us and Them. No matter where we find ourselves, where we work or what we do, there's that brutal separation of Us and Them – that, and the absence of love.

I'd like to return to the Land of Memories. It's like a longing for the womb as a safe, warm nest. Maybe I'm looking back at it through rose-tinted glasses. Often, there wasn't enough food there either, but everyone helped each other, everyone was on the same side. There was no Us and Them. Here, there's nothing except emptiness and oppression and the breaking of hearts. Such cruelty only breeds bitterness, and that can spread through people like a plague.

How did things change so suddenly? What went wrong? I question myself constantly, but there's no answer. All that the mind offers is a black hole.

HAGAR

Hagar was my sister, and she was with me through everything. I couldn't have been very old, nine summers at the most, and Hagar was a bit older than me. I don't know where Dad and Mum were at the time, but They came, dragged us out of bed, and forced us to march.

It's possible they would have left me behind, because Hagar was the one they really wanted. I was just a sgraggly thing, screaming the place down. But Hagar possesed beauty and grace, and everyone wanted to be her friend. That's the memory I have of her – of myself gripping on to her for dear life, holding on tightly to her dress of bright yellow material with black circles ... I remember her touch and her smell even now. As long as I didn't lose hold of her, I'd be safe.

But that night, Hagar was far from being safe, and they placed irons on her wrists, and a chain fixed to the irons, and we walked for days.

I thought I was used to being famished, but that was the first time for me to experience true hunger, a hunger that weakened me so much that I couldn't place one foot ahead of another. It was Hagar who helped me to walk. She would have carried me, had that been possible.

Instead, she told me stories, and that kept me going. Eventually, the long march came to an end and we were put in a prison for a number of days. At the time, we thought that this was the worst thing that could happen to us. But no. We had no idea of the real horror that awaited us when we were first taken prisoner in the Land of Memories. Before we realised it, we were chained to one another and taken aboard The Nightmare. We were so frightened we could smell our own fear as we were led up the gangway and then climbed down into the darkness that was the bowels of The Nightmare, down into the hell from which there was no return.

Hagar did her best to staunch my fears. All of this will pass, she told me. Don't listen to what other people say, don't listen to their stories ... to do so will only prolong the fear and the pain and the horror that will eventually be over. Hagar was right, because in truth we knew nothing of what lay ahead of us and all we could cling to was that little pearl inside us – that little pearl of hope, nestled somewhere inside us. "Listen to the song of the birds in your soul," Hagar said. "Guard that song and keep it close to your heart, guard every little pearl of remembering from home. In time they'll prove to be worth more than gold."

At the time, I believed her. But by now, any memory of the bird's song has sunk to the recess of my mind, but I held on to the image.

"You can teach yourself to remember," were Hagar's words at the time. "Every night, before you fall asleep over here after working in the burning hot fields, think of Mam and Dad and little Nague, and go from house to house in the village with them in your mind, naming everyone that you meet. In this way, you'll always remember. Because that's the hour, just before sleep, when they're with us in spirit, when our people back in the Land of Memories think of us and try to contact us in spirit – and we try our best to respond to their call. We should be trying to find a way to get back to them."

"How is this possible, Hagar," I asked, "now that we've been brought forcibly so far away from home, so far away that it'll be very difficult to ever find our way back again?"

"Believing that we can return is half the battle," Hagar said, and then added in an exhausted voice. "You'll come to understand in time."

Strange how her words have stayed with me, deep in my heart ever since. And not only her exact words, but the intonation of her voice and the look in her eyes. She wanted me hold onto hope above all else. And she was right too, of course. Hope is all that remains, when everything else that's yours has been stripped away and is gone – even your precious, beloved sister.

THE SLAVEOWNER AND THE CHATTEL

We were in the belly of The Nightmare for sixty days. It was the worst hell I've ever experienced. No one knew where they were taking us. Many of our fellow captives insisted that The Nightmare was crossing the oceans to the far end of the world where it would crash over the side and we'd all be killed. There was only thing everyone knew for sure – no one had ever returned once captured.

You wouldn't have believed how giant a ship The Nightmare was, even if I could have drawn a picture of it. You wouldn't have believed how many of us managed to crawl into the dark bowels of the vessel below deck. Human beings piled on top of one another, worse than animals. Wherever you looked, there were people lying on the cold timbers in every space and nook. The men were in chains, long chains attached to the beams. We were allowed to stretch just once a day when we were taken up onto the deck to get some air. Sometimes we'd have to dance to a violin accompaniment, like peforming monkeys, much to the delight of our masters. The image of those macabre dances will stay with me forever, our feet in the heavy chains raised an inch or two above the floor.

The worst thing was smelling the fresh air and the salt for just a few minutes each day, and then having to go back downstairs to face the terrible stink down below. Men with scarves over their faces climbed below deck to give us some food each day, but if you wanted to go to the toilet, you had to do so right there on the spot ... the stink and the filth was overwhelmingly appalling. I think this is what killed poor Hagar in the end. She caught some kind of infection or disease, and just faded away in the end, the poor thing.

And all the hours there in the guts of hell, we couldn't hold to anything firm or solid, this constant rolling back and forth and being thrown around on the waves all day long and the longer hours of night. The only time they released someone from their fetters was when they were dying. Out on deck, some captives tried to escape and leaped over the side-rails of the ship when they could endure no more misery and suffering. And the hunger was worse than anything, like a wild animal gnawing in your stomach. When I was so weak that I couldn't move, Hagar would give me her food. She was so generous and I shouldn't have taken it but the hunger pains forced me to. Should I have accepted her offers of food, I often think to myself these days? Is it my fault that Hagar is no longer here?

THE PLACE I NEVER GO

In my mind are a series of steps leading down into the vaults of memory. In my quiet moments, I venture down carefully, gripping the side-rails tightly. And eventually I always reach a door below – a door that looks closed tight. I can keep this door shut most of the time. But sometimes, when I'm sleeping or just in a spontaneous moment, I see myself walking towards the door and slowly turning the handle to open it. I know the pain that emerges from that room but I open it all the same, because I want to remember, even if it pains me.

And I always find Hagar there on the other side of the door. Hagar, my sweet sister who took care of me even before I learned to walk. Hagar taught me how to walk by holding my hand, helping me hesitantly put one foot in front of the other. Hagar was a like a mother to me; Hagar, she was my rock and my shield. I loved her and followed her every move ... to this day I can feel the cotton of her dress brushing against my skin, her fingers stroking my head.

And then at the end, as she grew weaker and weaker and her life was slipping away, it was me trying to look after her. The roles were reversed. It was me stroking her hair and talking to her softly as a child, as her life ebbed away. How many times in those last days did I tell her that she'd be all right, that things would be fine, and yet I never imagined she wouldn't be there to protect me. When her last breath came, I felt an incredible loneliness. The person I loved most in the world was gone. I'd never felt so completely alone.

The earth did not receive her. After she died, the masters just unceremoniously dumped her body into the ocean. Poor Hagar. When she died, half of me died with her. Now that Hagar has passed on, I can only draw on old memories of Mother, Father Dad and little Nague, and without Hagar they risk becoming imaginary characters in my mind. I can't mention their names to anyone anymore, either, as they don't mean anything to others. While Hagar was alive, I knew I wasn't fantasising. She was a living being, she was laughing eyes and a wide smile, it was fun to be in her company.

I long for her. I've made myself sad now, but I don't want to shut the door on her forever. I miss her so much.

THE DAY WHEN NOTHING HAPPENED

My job in the morning is to feed the pigs. I like this time of the day best of all, the early hours when it's just me and the morning light. Every day follows the same pattern but sometimes I say to myself as I carry their food down to the pens, "Maybe this is the day when the world will change. Maybe this is the day when freedom dawns." But if the day that we're set free ever comes, it'll surely begin the same as any other – the same light and the pigs as hungry as ever – whether it's Freedom Day or not. And maybe I'll see Phibah waving her arms from the house and smiling from ear to ear. And Hannibal running towards me and calling out in a breathless voice, "Haven't you heard? A row has broken out up at May Penn, something's finally happening!" And I'll ruck up my skirt and follow Hannibal as quickly as my legs can carry me. This morning there isn't a soul to be seen, however, and the pigs are squealing loudly for their food.

We spent all morning and afternoon cutting cane in the fields. It was tough work and my back and my hands were very sore at the end of day. We ate our evening meal and fell asleep with exhaustion. There was nothing unusual about today. No one was hurt and no one died, which made it a good day, I suppose. All I could say of the day is that it was "the day when nothing happened". This is another reason why this account can't be described as a diary in the true sense of the word – every day that passes is the same as the next.

A SMALL HOUSE IN A BIG HOUSE

When Phibah comes back from the Big House at the end of the day, we talk. She's a good few years older than me but we're friends all the same; she works in a different world, the world of the Big House. Because of this, she's likely to live to ten years longer than most of us here.

"Who cares? Who wants to live another ten years in this hell-hole?" asked Plato, but we didn't pay any attention to him. Plato is a bitter old man who never stops complaining about things.

Phibah works hard, but she's lucky that her hands aren't all disfigured and scarred, like mine. She works in the kitchen of the Big House, and this is one of the best jobs on this plantation, even better than a job such as a cleaner, for example. What she'd really love would be a job as a maid. Only those whose skin is brown or more coffee-coloured are allowed work in the Big House, however. And there's no shortage of such mixed-race people because the White Man has been rampantly raping so many women and spreading his seed.

"I wouldn't lower myself to serve and wait on the White Man," I said to Phibah one day.

"Don't act so righteous," she replied. "You already serve and wait when you're out cutting the sugar cane or feeding the pigs, or if you're a maid. Serving them is the sole purpose of your life."

"I couldn't be in their company, or help them get dressed, touch their skin, or pour them tea – the intimacy would disgust me beyond measure. Even breathing the same air as them is something I can't bear to imagine ..."

"I don't think of them as people at all," Phibah says one day. "It's that simple. To me they aren't human ... they're just creatures without heart or feeling – unlike you and me. Their world is a fantasy world."

Next she told us about something incredible that she'd witnessed while working in the Big House, something that she'd never seen before. Phibah said that the child in the Big House has a house in her room – a tiny house that's a miniature version of the Big House. There were different rooms in this tiny model house, and windows and doors that opened and closed like a real house. The rooms had furniture, a mat on the floor, a small table with little figurines and furniture the size of your thumbs ... I found it difficult to believe.

"Why would you have a tiny house in a real house?" I asked Phibah.

"So that the little girl can play with it," she replied, as if this were completely obvious.

How would the girl have time to play, I thought, before realising that everyone in the Big House – the children included – have all the time in the world. They have nothing to do all day, since we do all the work for them.

I couldn't imagine spending my days doing nothing. It was beyond me! Even as a small child I'd always been working, collecting water from the well, helping my mother with the cooking and cleaning, helping to wash clothes and looking after the elders.

To spend your day in the Big House playing with dolls. What a strange world! A small house inside the Big House!

"They have little dolls that fit insde this small house that they play with for fun. The dolls look exactly like them, the dolls in the small house are dressed the same as the people from the Big House," said Phibah with a smile, before adding, "and the dolls have nothing to do either!"

JONI GONAR

Some days weigh down on you, heavy with gloom and menace. You can feel it on the air even before the day's work has begun. It's as if the cane plants are whispering ominously to one another, telling tales that we don't want to hear.

We were cutting the cane and loading it onto carts when we heard loud shouts and screams coming from the far end. We were afraid to stop working but we knew immediately that something strange had happened. You could tell from the terror in the voices.

Severe beatings from the masters and the agonies of whip, young slaves like us dying well before their time, the ominous presence of death ... it almost becomes normal after a while in this hell. You can almost feel the evil presence in the air, like an invisible fog that wraps itself around you and makes you lose your sanity completely.

"What's happening?" I ask Prue who is working next to me in the field.

"Joni Gonar has appeared."

Joni Gonar! If someone had hit me with a hammer in that moment, we couldn't have been more shocked! Joni Gonar was a hero to us, a man who'd assumed almost mythical proportions. A giant of a man, seven-foot tall with a mass of wavy hair, his body covered with decoration. For two years, Joni Gonar had been assumed dead, his body never found following his break for freedom. Then, just six months after his disappearance, someone spotted Joni Gonar again somewhere on the outskirts of the plantations. The slavemasters, including Big Brute, went off to hunt him down. Two days later, they returned on their horses, dragging Joni Gonar behind them with ropes. Then they tortured him, branding his shoulder with a hot iron while cursing him with every name under the sun, taking it in turns to whip him with the lash and spitting on him. They whipped Joni Gonar dozens of times until rivers of blood flowed from his body all along the ground. No one could survive what they'd put Joni Gonar through, surely? No one could tolerate such pain?

But Joni Gonar refused to yield. He refused to die until his torturers became frightened and ran away. And for a second time, Joni Gonar escaped and went on the run and became a hero to us forever. To escape the plantation once was an incredible feat – but to do it for a second time and evade his pursuers, intent on death, was something completely magical. We knew for certain that they'd kill him if they ever caught Joni Gonar again. But they never did. He evaded all his pursuers and his status as our hero was restored. Some people claimed to have witnessed his second escape. They said that a great eagle had swooped down from the heavens, and a bloodied and battered Joni had climbed onto its back and flown away to freedom. Others again claimed that Joni Gonar himself had turned into an eagle and disappeared, never to be the seen again. Either way, Joni became the stuff of legend, the first person to have challenged the White Man and defeated him. Just the mention of his name gave everyone a feeling of hope, ever afterwards.

But this morning, the myth of Joni Gonar came to a very sad end. It was unclear how they'd captured him this time but capture him they did. And this time they'd ensure that he would neither run nor walk again. There would be no more talk of escape. The slavemasters and the overseer dragged Joni Gonar out into the yard of May Penn and branded his other shoulder with the hot iron. And this time, they cut off his foot with a long knife and the soil ran red with Joni Gonar's blood. With his body not whole, they know that Joni Gonar can never return to the Land of Memory, and there's no more escape for him. Joni Gonar, the man, has been destroyed. Joni Gonar the man and the legend is no more.

And in case anyone doesn't believe me, I have seen poor Joni Gonar there in the yard with my own two eyes. I saw Joni Gonar lying there with one good leg and the other a bloodied stump of flesh. And I heard a small boy who witnessed him also ask his mother – one of the servants – in a trembling voice: "Is that Joni Gonar, Mum?"

"That was Joni Gonar," was his mother's grim response, leading her child away.

FORTUNE

Whenever I have a few minutes free from work, there's nothing I enjoy more than spending time with one of the children. This always raises my spirits. One of these children is Fortune. Fortune is too small to do much work yet, but he hates to be idle. Fortune even has his own small knife to cut the cane. His greatest fear is losing this knife and being punished for this.

I feel very protective of him. If I was offered anything in this world, what I'd most like to do is remove the fear from Fortune's eyes. He has a smile of wonder that illuminates his face, but the fear never disappears completely from his eyes.

His mother Maia does the same work as us harvesting the cane and we take turns to keep an eye on Fortune. Maia is seven months pregnant and has a lot of trouble bending and lifting during work. We all help one another when we can.

"Are you alright, Fortune?" I ask the little boy one late afternoon.

"I'm tired," he says.

"Do you want me to sing a song for you?"

"Maybe we can sing together?"

"Of course. What about 'Thula Thula' – at peace, little child'? I began to sing ... and although the heat was overwhelming and we were dripping with perspiration, the song sustained us and gave us comfort.

"Tula tula tula baba,
Tula tula tula sana,
Tula tula tula baba,
Thula thula thula san."

We sing together for a short until I hear someone call my name.

"Ebony!"

It was Clara who came running.

"It's Maia. She's not well."

"I thought we had someone helping her on the cane this afternoon."

"We had, but we were afraid to leave our row or to go more slowly," Clara says.

"Let's slow down now anyway. You can't do everything. I'll make sure that the rest of us here go more slowly – we'll try to do it without the overseer noticing."

Fortune was standing next to me now, holding my hand.

"Maia's collapsed!" someone shouted suddenly from two rows away and Fortune held me even more tightly. He gave my hand a squeeze and then let go again. I could tell that he wanted to run away, but I stopped him. I had a very bad feeling about this. I crouched down on the ground and stared into his eyes.

"Fortune – you must stay with me! You have to be a very good boy now, and keep working and your mammy will be fine. Alright?"

Fortune looked into the distance.

"Look, Big Brute's coming. Do you think he'll help?"

My heart sank on seeing this beast approach on his horse. He must have noticed the commotion between the rows of cane. By now, a number of girls and women had stepped out from their work furrows and circled Maia who was writhing on the ground with pain.

"We'll have to move her. We can't leave her here in the heat like this," says Anna.

"Can someone keep Fortune away so he's not too upset?"

Big Brute came closer. By the time he reached us, he was off his horse and walking through the ridges. He saw Maia on the floor and gave a grunt of disgust. He told her to get up twice but when she didn't respond, he drew his whip, then shouted to one of the men to dig a hole in the soil. And Poor Maia suffered the same fate as other pregnant woman did. He dragged her to her knees and made her lie face-down in the hole the man had dug, then whipped her mercilessly. At the crack of the whip, everyone went silent with horror. I grabbed Fortune's shoulders and looked him straight in the eye. I hoped he wasn't old enough to realise what was going on, but by his look, I could tell he understood exactly what was happening. I'd never seen so much pain in anyone's eyes.

I gestured to him to keep quiet, not to say anything, and he did what I said. I watched the hot tears fill his eyes and stream down his face. And in that moment, I hated this evil system of slavery more than anything else in the world. And I hated my powerlessness to do anything about this inhuman system even more. The only thing I could to stand up to this brutality was to try and stop a small child screaming because his own mother was being punished. After Big Brute finished lashing her, he had one of the men drag her, bloodied and beaten, out of the hole. Our only hope was that the little one in her womb had survived and would come into the world in a few month's time unscathed. The poor creature. At least the unborn child had already had a taste of the harsh treatment that awaited him in this world.

THE SECRET

I thought it'd just happened to me and nobody else. I was so ashamed that I couldn't bring myself to tell anyone about it – not a soul. And it was only when I fell into conversation with Belinda coming in from the fields one day that I discovered I wasn't alone. In truth, I wasn't that fond of Belinda. A tall and hard-looking woman with cold, sparkling eyes, I didn't like the way she looked at me and I was suspicious of her. She wasn't much older than me but she was far taller than I was and far more developed physically than me.

As we trooped in from work one evening she fell in beside me and asked if she could talk to me. Initially I was unsure and asked her why she'd come to me.

"The other girls have noticed what's happening to you," she said.

I was shocked! I thought that I'd hidden my pain from the others. Before I knew it, I was unburdening myself to Belinda of my terrible secret.

It had started just a few months earlier, I told her. Big Brute had come up to me one day and ordered me to follow him. I was afraid he was about to whip me, and my heart was in my mouth. Inside his cabin, he began stroking my hair and body and told me to lie on the table. And he did things to me then, things that I had no comprehension of. Up until then, I thought that at least my body was my own but I found out differently that day. These people take everything from you – every single thing on this Earth! I'd never told anyone about it before and suddenly I found myself weeping.

"He did the same to me," said Belinda.

Oh my God! I was shocked. I managed to manage staunch my tears and recover myself.

"I thought it was better than being whipped, but I'm not sure that it is, to be honest. Not once or twice, but it's continued regularly for weeks now."

Belinda nodded and I knew she understood exactly what I meant.

"I don't know how to stop him," I said, my eyes filling with tears again.

"There's no way of stopping him, Ebony. We just have to live with it. It won't last forever. He'll go after other women in due course, and it'll be their turn then."

Was that really any comfort to us – that the pain and abuse would be passed onto someone else when he'd got tired of us?

"Like you, I thought I was the only one for a long time – until I heard the other women talking one night," Belinda said, "and someone mentioned you. The others were afraid to say anything, but I thought it would be better to tell you what happened to me. There's nothing as terrible as trying to cope with it alone."

"Thank you, Belinda."

"It's another way they have of despising us. Whatever you do, the most important thing of all is that you stay strong. Always remember however, they can do what they like with our bodies, but they can never take our mind or soul from us," she said afterwards.

I viewed Belinda in a new light after this, and considered her my friend. And this was when I realised that comfort can be found in the most unexpected of places.

THE SAME THING OVER AND OVER

I struggle to get up in the mornings sometimes. Maybe this is a sign that I'm moving into adulthood. When I was a little girl, I remember waking up in the morning and feeling the excitement of a new day ahead.

Sometimes, in the Land of Memories, I woke up before everyone else and ventured to the door. Although I didn't dare step over the threshold and go outside until we were ordered to do so, I often opened the door and sat there for a while, taking in the beauty of late-dawn. Some mornings, Hagar came looking for me and sat down beside me. We wouldn't say a word to one another but just sit there and enjoy the fact that no one else was awake or watching us. There's a special feeling in the air at this time of the day, and we enjoyed watching the light slowly wake to the living world before beginning our work for the day. The first to person to come into view was always Yusan and his goats, and once he had passed by, we knew that it was time for everyone to wake up.

Other times, it was the cock crowing loudly that woke me from the depths of sleep. I think back to my early days in the Land of Memories when, still lying in bed, I watched my mother preparing food for the entire family. She'd send me out to get some water and I'd walk down to the end of the village, past Garbi's chickens scratching at the dry earth and Toro's house where the children would be outside playing jumping and skipping games in the early light. I remember one little boy who greeted me every day and asked where I was off to. It was the game we played each day for fun – the same question and response – but it was a game we enjoyed playing.

This is the big difference between here and the Land of Memories. Back home, there was both a pattern and a purpose to our every living day. Here on the plantation, there's a pattern but no obvious purpose to our long hours of daily work. Neither I nor anyone understand the purpose of all of this. The work here continues hour after hour while there's still daylight. It's never-ending. We work for the White Man, without pay and without rest. And if this is all that life is, hour by hour until we fall into the grave, I hope that I don't live too long. I'd rather have stayed a child forever, a child with dreams and hopes in the Land of Memories.

The White Man believes there's only one god, and they believe that he once lived here on Earth (as a white man, needless to say). There are no black people in their religion that we know of. This world is a world of suffering, and the important thing is order – to work and to obey. Once someone's dead, they go to a place called Heaven, or a place of terrible suffering called Hell. There's nowhere worse than Hell, they say. But we all know it's the other way around really. That here is the real Hell, and that Heaven is Africa. That's why the Boiler House is known as Hell. It doesn't matter what part of the plantation you work in, the hours are brutal and hard and the work kills us slowly (or very quickly, at times). The biggest torture of all is that there's no escape from the endless hours of toil. We have no choice. Even after all the years of work, our lot hasn't improved at all. Actually, it gets worse.

Even the people who live the longest here mean nothing to them. All of us are just an unit of production to them, an item of value that's to be exploited until we're skin and bone and nothing else. And here I am – a growing woman – and I've nothing to look forward to in life, just the realisation that my life will gradually get tougher and harsher over time. Time running down in work and more work until death comes calling sooner or later ... the same thing over, day after day, week after week, year upon year.

FEEDING THE BEAST

The work with the machines, the Hell – is a very dangerous place. One mistake and you can be critically injured or killed. I rarely have to go there to feed the cane into the big metal machines, thank God, as the conditions there are lethal. It's the constant rush with which the slavemasters make us work that causes these problems. Once the cane is cut and shredded it has to be put through the machines quickly so that the juices can be extracted. Otherwise they go dry and hard and they're worthless. And the slavemasters go crazy when this happens and the whips come out! They constantly demand that we work faster and faster.

The machine we feed the cane into has huge metal jaws and is like a great monster with an insatiable appetite. We call it the Beast. And a few weeks ago, while feeding the Beast, there was a terrible accident. Mirtilla's hands got caught in the machine and she lost both her arms! There's nothing more useless (or more sad) in this world than the servant who's been crippled, or left without their arms or limbs. They sent Mirtilla to the hospital and staunched the blood, but they say that where her arms once were, she'll be left with nothing but two stumps. She says her arms hurt her terribly, even though they're not there anymore. As far as the masters are concerned, she's useless to them now; she's nothing more than a burden on their time and resources, another mouth to feed.

A few weeks later, we slaves did something that we've never done before. Someone came up with the idea of coming together to sing and play music, and so we organised a small concert for Mirtilla. Once the work was done for the day, we gathered outside the hut that Mirtilla has lain in since the accident, and we got hold of any bits of timber and boxes that we could beat out some rhythms on. It turned out to be a very special night. Beating out our rhythms and songs in the darkness, we felt a sense of unity and solidarity that we hadn't felt before. We carried Mirtilla out to the door of her hut, and we wept and sang and danced with her for hours. We finally felt as one. Only when the Overseer appeared on his horse and shouted at us did we go home. I'll never forget that night where everyone came together. And even if she didn't sing, Mirtilla was with us and was one of us, and we were acting as her friend and protector in a strange and powerful way. Music is something incredibly powerful. It's a form of healing.

BAD OMENS

Every day, as I harvest the cane I try to channel my
anger and frustration into the cutting knife that's in my
hand. With every stroke, it's as if I'm fighting back
against them, fighting back against the masters and the
system. This is the only way I can maintain my self-
respect and keep my spirits up. I think of all of us who've
been whipped or crushed or broken. I think of everyone
who's been killed or who's died because of the brutality
of the overseers and slavemasters. Every time I use my
machete and hack the cane plants, I name everyone and
everything we've lost, the torments we've suffered – my
own sufferings in my young life up to now. Leaving home
– hack, losing Hagar – hack, the lack of food – hack, Big
Thug – hack, all their hate towards us – hack, hack, hack.
It's a battle between Us and Them, every hour of every
day, and physical exhaustion is their greatest weapon
against us. Because this is how they triumph over us at
end of each day. Endless work and physical exhaustion is
the invisible chain they use to keep us captive. We're
captives as the sun sets each evening and as the dawn
breaks on every new day. The sole small triumph that's
ours, as we stumble home from the fields each evening,
is that we're still alive. Another day has passed and
they haven't crushed us completely. We're still alive,
we're still fighting, even if the battle is still more a battle
of the mind than the body. Oh, How I hate our

slavemasters and oppressors! If only we could strike back!

Mirtilla is dead. They found her in the lake at the back of the plantation, floating face downwards. No one knows if she drowned accidentally, or if she jumped in. No one will ever know. All we know is that she's gone. I'm glad that Mirtilla escaped.

There's something ominous on the breeze again. We feel it stalking us, strange and sinister. There are bad omens.

THE LOST KNIFE

It began with Fortune losing his cane-cutting knife. He had to borrow a bigger knife, and what did the Overseer do but hand him something that was far too heavy and unwieldy for him, and more like a machete than a knife. This heavy chopping knife got tangled in the canes and Fortune let it fall by accident, causing a deep gash in his leg just below the knee. When he saw what'd happened to Fortune, Nero exploded with anger and shook his knife in Big Thug's face. Poor Nero suffered a flogging for this. Titus and Quasha went beserk too, and were also punished with the whip. Sometimes, it's impossible to put up with so much brutality and hate without going crazy yourself. Fortune blames himself for what happened because if he hadn't mislaid his knife, the others wouldn't have found themselves on the ground, battered and bleeding.

Nero and Titus and Quasha are now all locked in the cellar of the Big House. Big Brute is an animal with his whip. And yet they never seem to understand – the more they use the lash on us, the worse things will get. The more they persecute us and abuse us, the more they hasten their own demise. They're so brutal with us now that things are bound to boil over sooner or later.

There's a lot of anger and discontent amongst the people here. Rebellion is in the air. It's only a matter of time. Titus is whipped again – publicly this time. He's tied to a pole out in the yard. The Overseer rubs honey into his wounds to attract insects and torture him even more. Titus begins to moan and weep strangely. It's as if his body has gone numb with the pain and he's weeping from memory.

As if this wasn't bad enough, they went to fetch Plato. They unwrapped the rope that had tied Titus to the pole and shoved him onto the ground on his back, with two of the Big Thugs holding him down. Then they forced his mouth open and under threat of the lash they made Plato open his trousers and piss on Titus' face. What a disgusting and animalistic thing to do while forcing men, women and children to watch! How low can these beasts go? Anyone who tried to avert their eyes or refuse to watch felt the lash. I can feel the hatred in me, eating me like a cancer.

THE LASH

I felt the lash myself today. All I did was rest for a moment. My arms were numb from exhaustion and I could barely lift them.

'Let things be' were the words I heard myself say. 'Rest a moment, be gentle with yourself,' I imagined a smiling Hagar saying to me. It felt strange just to put down my cutting knife for a moment, to close my eyes and remember how much Hagar loved me. 'Listen to the bird song in your soul' – that's what Hagar used to say.

The birds flew away at incredible speed today.

Because my eyes were still closed, I never noticed Big Brute sneak up behind me and produce the whip. Before I knew it, I felt my back smart and burn with the strokes of his lash. I never imagined it'd hurt so badly. My back shuddered with the force of his every stroke and I fell face downwards onto the ground. I felt my skin tear and bleed and I screamed in agony. Yes, the physical pain is horrific, but the contempt and shame you feel as a human being is almost as strong. The fact that they believe we're just animals, or less than animals, and that they have the right to treat us this way ... After the whipping, Big Brute insisted that I get up off the ground and continue with my work. I couldn't – I hadn't an ounce of strength left in my body. They dragged me away and locked me in the cellar of one of the buildings here instead.

I should probably be grateful that I can't work at the moment as I'd surely be dead by now if I hadn't collapsed after the whipping, but I can't relax. I'm too afraid of what they might do to me next. My fear of them is eating away inside of me and I can barely eat the scraps of food they give here. I feel weak and dizzy, as if I'm about to collapse at any moment again. I count the scars on my hands and arms and see how the skin has become leathery and hard like an old woman's. And yet the rough clothes we wear each day still hurt and torment our broken skin. Our slave clothes, the same thing we wear all year long. Once the year ends – if you're still alive by then, of course – they give you another costume made of the same rough material, and exactly the same colour.

I can't remember how it felt to wear anything else by now. Was I born wearing these clothes? There's a hole in the right-hand side of my dress and I've tried to mend it many times. It's been torn again and the hole has got worse. The thread I've used to mend my dress is made of a different colour to the material ... I wonder whose fingers wove the flannel and clothes we wear here? What kind of people were they? Were they slaves like us, slaves from somewhere else in the world? In another world, in an imaginary paradise, I swap my work in the fields for sewing clothes. There's something comforting about the idea of sitting with needle and thread in hand and creating something new, and perhaps working in the company of other women.

The Overseer wears different clothes from one week

to the next. Only rarely have I seen his wife and children, but they're like people from a different world, his young daughters sporting pretty light cotton blouses and dresses made of different colours. I remember Hagar's dress, still – it was yellow with black circles ... There must have been a time when I wore clothes other than these horrible slave uniforms, when I had something soft and sweet next to my skin.

My thoughts were interrupted by the sound of someone moving outside the cellar. I froze with with fear.

"Who's there?" a voice whispers in the dark.

"Me ... it's me! Ebony."

"Ebony! What are you doing here? You're too young to cause trouble! Why you?"

I tell the voice what happened to me.

"There's talk of escape," whispers the voice.

"From here, from the cellar?"

"No, no! From this place, a real escape from this hell – from here – from the plantation."

On hearing this, I felt as if someone had kicked me in the stomach. Escape! Escape the same as Joni Gonar tried more than once? What's wrong with them? They must be crazy. We'd end up the same as poor Joni Gonar. We'd never get out alive. They'd hunt us down in no time.

"Escape and not being caught again. That's where Joni Gonar went wrong!" whispers the voice.

"Yes, but the poor man didn't choose to be caught."

"If we escaped, we'd make sure we were never caught."

Escape? I repeated this word in my mind until it found sanctuary there. The thought of escape – just the thought of it – escape, never to return ...!

I dared myself to repeat this forbidden word until I thought it might set my mouth on fire. I wanted to play with it, sip it, blow it out like a bubble, silently, over and over again, until this magical word – escape – echoed in my mind ... Because, if I was to be honest, this was the only thing that made sense.

SWEETNESS

I'm back in the fields cutting the cane again. My body cries out with pain, the muscles that had tasted rest for those few short days burning with agony. Keep moving. Keep hacking and cutting. Hack hack! Chop chop, chop! Keep going. Keep working until you drop.

I've been doing this work for so long now. How much sugar cane have I cut at this stage? Where does the fruit of all our slave-work go? There are so many of us doing the same job across the vast plantations here. And there never seems to be an end to it. Week on week, they take more land and cultivate it, and plant more and more cane. Is there any end to this world of cane, this world of sugar? None of us have ever eaten sugar, so it isn't necessary for living – it's not the essence of life and it's possible to live without it.

But from what we hear from the Big House, the wealthy people take the sugar one spoonful at a time and use it to sweeten a cup of tea or coffee, to give them energy. It's fashionable now amongst the rich across many countries, they say.

If they take the sugar one spoonful at a time, imagine how many thousands or millions of people are in richer countries, every one of them with his cup and spoon ... the world must be a huge place. Phibah says that they use the sugar in the Big House. She tasted it once but didn't like it. She says that it's far sweeter than any banana or any other fruit she's ever tasted, sweeter than honey itself. The rich people in the Big House don't have drinking vessels like ours, Phibah said. Their cups are different, with delicate handles shaped like ears that they hold with their fingers. And they place a saucer underneath the cup to catch any drops that fall. Maybe I'll see them drinking tea or coffee some day up at the Big House.

When I think of how close the Big House is to our huts, and yet how different their lives are from ours ...

FOOD

At night, having something to eat is one of the few
opportunities we have to socialise with one another.
We're always so hungry by mealtimes. I can't remember
now what food we ate in the Land of Memories, but I like
listening to some of the older people describe African
food and how much better the food was there – 'real
food', as they say. Different fruits and vegetables and
their unique smells and flavours. Their eyes just come
alive at the memory of this food. Sometimes, they'll
recall a wedding feast that took place, or the food that
people shared on a festival day, and it can brings tears
to their eyes. They speak so fondly of such times that I
too miss them, even if I have little memory of those days
now! How wonderful it is to long for that which you have
but faint memories. It's almost a tribal memory that we
seek to share with one another so far away from our real
homes. There are people among us here who were born
in Africa, but there are many who were born here also;
irrespective of this, we all share the nostalgia for the
Land of Memories.

There's a wide range of African people amongst us
here, people of different groups and tribes, including
those who never tasted some of the exotic foods the
elders remember. But even the food of the poorest
people back home had more flavour to it than what they
give us to eat here – all the older people can confirm

this. Here, there's no gentry or hierarchy amongst us. We're all on the same level as rats, even if that's the lowest level of humanity in the eyes of our slavemasters – we're all equal and as one when amongst ourselves. It's only in the smallest things that the differences amongst us as people manifest themselves – the way we look or talk or eat, or even the way we hold ourselves when walking. In truth, I'm glad that I don't remember many aspects of life from when we were stolen from the Land of Memories. Such sweet and beautiful memories would prove too painful to bear.

HAPPINESS

I laughed today. Clara was collecting the dishes on one end of the table, and I collected them at the other end. We brought the two piles together, and we almost dropped them all on the floor! I thought she was catching them, and she thought I was going to do it. For a moment we look at one another in pure horror. But then the mistake is realised, and here we are, holding them tight, laughing with relief perhaps, both of us ... that was an odd experience. And we couldn't stop. Others turned to look at us, smiling. It was such a nice feeling. And I realised how much time had gone since I had laughed. Living without laughter is a cruel form of bondage. Everyone should be free to laugh.

LANGUAGE

Sometimes I think back to when we were forced to leave Africa forever. Back to when the slavemasters captured us and forced us into the hellhole ship that was The Nightmare. The great silence below deck. The silence of not knowing what lay ahead of us, or whether we would survive the horrific journey. The silence that comes with resignation and praying for death as our release. The silence of people falling sick and collapsing and fading into the final terrible silence of death.

I don't remember how we spoke to one another in those first days below deck. With our eyes and the movement of our hands and with some sort of sign language, I suppose. As the ship held different tribes and peoples, we didn't understand other people's languages, depending on where they'd come from. And I think that most of us were too traumatised to speak much, anyway. It was just Hagar and the others from our tribe that I could communicate with. There was no need to understand what the White Man was saying – his language was the language of grunts and violence. When he shouted and roared, we didn't need to understand his words; it was enough to understand the hatred and contempt in his voice. Gradually, we came to learn the White Man's language, or at least the gist of it. When someone hears the same barked orders and instructions each day, they come to understand quickly enough.

We captives came to understand one another over time, even if I'm not sure how this happened, exactly. It was as if we put each other's words into a pot and stirred them carefully for a long time until we came to a new form of understanding. When it came to the songs and music, we understood one another from the very beginning, however. There's nothing quite like song or music to bring people together. Initially, we sang whenever we felt happy and wished to celebrate or give thanks. But now, we sing all the time, even when there's nothing to celebrate or no cause for joy. We sing now to give comfort or a sense of calm, and we also sing to express anger and pain. We sing to keep our memories alive and to give words to hope. You can do anything with song – from calming a baby to encouraging someone to fight. Songs and music can help you to remember and they can help you to forget. Sometimes, someone strikes up a tune when we're working and we join in and everyone sings the chorus. Sometimes we sing verses in response to one another, like a game or a way to make the time pass more quickly.

Slowly, we learned one another's songs and came to understand one another as people. We learned to sing with one voice.

FRIGHTENED OF WHAT IS TO COME

Rumours of rebellion are going around. I've said that I'm definitely not interested in trying to escape, but if the entire plantation rebels the others say that they'll have to take their chances. Some of the sick or those who've suffered beatings or injuries will need to be helped onto horses or carried in wheelbarrows or something. We'll have to push them or carry them away whatever way we can, just to get out of here, whatever form of escape presents itself at the time ... But the thought of them shooting us with their guns makes me very frightened.

THE VOICE OF MEMORY

It happened again. In my dreams, I found myself back in the Land of Memories and it was a thing of incredible beauty. I woke up before the others and listened to the Earth outside, its unusual silence. I felt myself in the place that's between sleep and waking, and I could hear the sounds of Home and my lost youth so clearly. In my dream, I could hear the sweet cries of the birds, remembering the shuffling of Mum's feet on the floor. The sounds and smells of food being prepared, the sounds of the kitchen and home. I hope I'll be able to store these sounds in my memory forever as they're an endless source of comfort to me. These are what I still have when everything else has been taken from me.

There are things I can't remember – Mum's voice or Dad's – sadly, they're long gone. But I still remember Hagar's voice very clearly. That's something. Her voice is always with me, burned into my soul, like the mark that says 'slave' that's branded on my skin that will never leave me.

In the early dawn hours, when the world is somewhere between wake and sleeping, and dreams have yet to complete their journey, this is the time for remembering, the time to hear the sights and sounds of home.

DISASTER DAY

A mess of a day. Everything fell apart. After imagining Freedom Day for so long, I'd thought of it as one sudden occassion. But it's a series of rumours, and there's no sequence to them.

However, it's not one occassion that stays in my mind for that day, just yet another tragedy.

Maia hasn't been well since she received that unmerciful beating. It's as if a light has disappeared from her life, as if something inside her has died. She was forced tried to go back to working in the fields but she was too weak. In the end, they moved her into the Big House to do various jobs in the kitchens there. Poor Fortune was still working with us out with the canes, but he was obviously very concerned about his mother.

"Mum's not well," he said to me one day, and I had no choice but to agree with him. How could I deny something that was so obvious? We hear some news about Maia from Phibah, but what we hear doesn't bode well.

Then one day Lydia came to me and said that Maia had given birth to her baby, but things hadn't gone well. The baby hadn't lived for very long, and Maia herself had nearly died during the birth. We spent the night chanting and praying to the gods to save both mother and baby. In the end, Maia had escaped this world to be with her baby, and maybe this was for the best. Except that poor little Fortune has been left an orphan. Seeing the emptiness in his young eyes hurts even more than anything ... I didn't hear him laugh ever again.

Why would you want to bring a child into such a world as this?

THIS DAY WAS TO BE A DAY OF FREEDOM

Nero rushed over to me. "Ebony! They're coming! Quick, Eb-on-y!"

I was on my knees in the field hacking at the cane stalks having just heard about poor Maia, and I couldn't cope with someone shouting at me or rushing towards me. I was rooted to the ground – I just couldn't move, I was that upset. It was like I'd withdrawn back, retreating and curling into the comfort of the womb. Nero was insistent, however. I could see the excitement and the fear in his eyes. The revolt had begun. I watched as about thirty people, both men and women, came running across the fields, having downed tools. No, there were more – there must have been fifty people, at least.

"Come on, Ebony... it's time! Let's go! Do you hear me?!" Nero repeated as others rushed past. "It's happening, Ebony, it's happened."

I didn't know what he was talking about at first. I just wanted him to go away and leave me alone. He crouched down by my side.

"What's wrong with you? Let's go ... What is it? You look half-dead, girl, like you've seen a ghost or something!"

"Maia is dead." When I heard myself say these words, it was as if I was reciting a very ancient curse. I felt the tears well up in my eyes and I began to weep.

Nero raised his arm as if to fend off an imaginary foe, and then he hugged me.

"I'll carry you, Ebony ... anything to get you out of here. You have to come straight away, please ... I beg you, there's no time to lose!"

"Go, Nero ... You go, let me be. Go. I want to ..."

He grabbed my arm.

"You must come!"

"I'm sorry but I don't want to leave Fortune here by himself!"

I'll never forget Nero's face, the pain and confusion all rolled into one. I realised then that I meant more to him than I had ever thought.

"Please, Nero! Leave! Go! Quickly, Nero!"

And he was gone and I remember staring at his back, unsure as to whether I'd ever see him again. And Freedom Day or not, my feet remained rooted to the earth as hundreds of people ran past me, even if everything had changed.

MASSACRE OF THE INNOCENTS

Today was a disaster – a slaughter of innocent people! What should have been Freedom Day turned into something else completely. A horror unimaginable. So many of our people have been killed, their bodies left hanging on the wire fences and stakeposts as a warning to the rest of us, the vultures picking their bones clean. The terrible smell in our nostrils. The stench of blood and death. I'm so frightened that I can't sleep.

It wasn't us who initiated the rebellion. It was the others at Monkey Point, those poor souls who'd reached the end of their tether and made a break for freedom. The revolt went from one plantation to the next. It was like a storm moving from one place to another, and it reached us. There will be bloody retribution for what has happened. They'll take their revenge on those of us who are left – we will pay the price.

And if the Overseer was bad before, he's a hundred times worse now, like a rabid dog eager for revenge. Rumour has it that both Titus and Nero were killed, along with about one hundred others. I'm so numb with shock that I can't even cry. It's like I'm gone beyond feeling now with the horror of it all.

Hannibal was completely innocent and didn't take part in the attempted escape, but it makes no difference to them. A number of axes and knives were found missing from the warehouse, and it was he who got the blame.

Hannibal was dragged out into the square next to the Big House again and we were all forced to watch as he was tortured and lashed. We waited for the sound of the lash but it never came.

I try to forsee whatever suffering that may come our way, but I never imagined what was to come this time. Hannibal was placed on his back on the ground, and two of the Big Thugs forced him to open his mouth. Roger – of all people – was dragged to stand above him, and his trousers were taken down.

"NOOO!!!!" screamed Roger defyingly, and he was lashed across his face. When he fell to the floor, he was whipped so relentlessly that it was hard to recognise him. He wasn't more than raw meat. Sancho was then dragged forth, and bared. I could see that he was shaking. What followed is almost too loathsome to tell. Sancho had to crouch above Hannibal's face and shit into his mouth. I bowed my head in shame on Sancho's behalf, for Hannibal, and for every single one of us. The White Man had insulted us all.

We were forced to raise our heads and we were prohibited from closing our eyes. When Sancho was dragged away, a rag was tied over Hannibal's mouth so that he couldn't spit the dirt out. His wrists were placed in irons and his feet tied to a post. Four hours went by before they untied the rag over his mouth.

What kind of animal punishes a man in such a way?

LAST HOURS ON EARTH

Phibah is very low. She's was seriously injured when the trouble started. The Overseer had rushed through the kitchen with his gun, and ran past Phibah as she was removing a pot of water from over the open fire. The boiling water splashed over her bare arms, her face and her chest, and she was badly burned. But it's the shock that has affected her body and mind the worst of all. Since early dawn, Phibah has lain stretched out on the floor in her hut, delirious with the pain. I try my best to comfort her.

I've no medicine with which to relieve her pain. In her delirium, Phibah thinks that she's back in Africa, that she's young again. As soon as the first rays of light make their way across the earthen floor of the hut, she tells me where to get the leaves for the herbal mixture that'll ease the burns. But because she's feverish and in such agony, she thinks that we can find these herbs in the fields here when this isn't so. Back Home, her village in the Land of Memories teemed with trees and plants of every description. But here, the ground is hard and arid, and the only thing the slavemasters permit anyone to grow here is sugar cane. The Earth is angry with us because of the evil going on here and it's dry and barren as a consequence.

"Water ..." Phibah moans. "Water, please," she cries. I'd give anything for us to be able to spirit her back to the Aida Valley and ease her pain. But the Land of Memories is too far away now and there's nothing I can do for her here.

Phibah drifts painfully between sleep and waking for the rest of the morning. All I can do is sit by her side and hold her hand in an effort to comfort her as best I can. The threads on my sleeve are worn and are hanging loose. I tried to make a knot in it last week, so that it wouldn't unravel more, but I allow my idle fingers to fidget with it. I study the weave of the dress and notice how it's frayed. It used to be sturdy material, but months of wear has worn it down.

"Ebony, can I have a drop of water?"

Phibah is burning with fever and I have to get her some water. I don't have a drop to give her. We weren't allowed near the huts during the day.

"Water ... please ... just a little!" Phibah moans and cries. Her lips are so dry and her tongue is like sand. Her temperature is so high. I really have to try and cool her down. Maybe I could tear a bit of my sleeve and use it as a cooling cloth on her forehead.

"Phibah, I have to leave you for a short while. I'll be back as quickly as possible, in a few minutes I hope ... and I'll have something for you to drink, I promise."

I know where there will be water. It means taking a big risk but I can't sit here any longer looking on helplessly as Phibah suffers. I venture up to the door of the Big House; I've never stood in front of this door before. I'm frightened out of my wits, but I have no choice.

My heart is in my mouth as I rap on the door. To my

amazement, a young girl opens it, dressed in a white cotton uniform.

"You shouldn't be here," the small girl says in a surprised voice.

"Do you know Phibah?" I ask her.

"Phibah isn't here. She's sick and confined to her cabin."

"I know, I know. I'm looking after her at the moment. She lives right next to us"

The expression on the girl's face changes. She gives me a careful stare and glances left and right to see if anyone is listening to us.

"How is the poor creature?"

"She's not good. She needs water and I'm not supposed to call in here – ever!"

"You're taking a big chance, girl! Stay right there, and I'll see if I can get you some. Hand me your bowl!"

This was how I found myself standing outside the Big House and heard the voice of the slavemaster's daughter, playing, imitating the sound of someone groaning with pain.

"There you are – one, two, three!"

"No, no, Miss, no – it really hurts. Agh! It hurts so much!"

I peered through the hedge and was amazed at what I saw. A little fair-skinned girl with blonde hair tied back with pink ribbons. Was this her ... the Overseer's daughter? I'd heard about her but I'd never seen anyone dressed in such wonderful and expensive-looking clothes. The most disturbing thing about the scene was the luxuriously-dressed miniature dolls she was playing with.

She had dipped one of the dolls in black ink and then pretended to beat the doll on the back and shoulders.

"Now, now, that's against the rules! You're a bad woman and you need to be beaten!"

"Agh, agh!"

The girl made the sounds of the dolls being whipped and beaten.

"Hey!"

It was the maid who'd returned with the water bowl.

"Here you are. I've filled it for you. You best get away from here quickly in case anyone sees you. And tell Phibah I was asking for her. What happened to her was terrible. My name is Deliah ..."

"Thank you so much, Deliah."

Off I went, but I couldn't forget that little girl and her dolls, no matter what I did. The sight of her playing, pretending to curse and whip the tiny black doll; it had shattered my idea of childhood innocence.

While passing the stables, I spotted one of the Big Thugs, the one who'd raped me and punished me with the lash, making his way across the yard and dragging a reluctant Prue behind him. I almost let the water-bowl fall when I saw him staring at me. He asked what I was doing there, and I told him.

"I could whip you for that," the Big Brute said with a broad sneer, looking me up and down from head to toe as if judging an animal. He followed me into the hut, while still gripping Prue tightly, her arms trapped behind her back.

"Phibah has been very sick since the burning she suffered recently. I'm afraid that she's dying."

"Hmph!" Big Brute said with a sneer. "It'd be better for all of us if she was gone. She's useless for anything now, anyway – just a worthless thing. She's nothing but skin and bone ... just a skeleton. But look at this frisky, healthy little thing I've come across here now," he says, dragging a struggling Prue out in front of him.

I lowered my head and stared at the ground in shame.

"Look at me when I address you!" he barked at me.

I couldn't bear to look at Prue, knowing full well what sort of abuse she was facing now. I could feel the tears well up in my eyes.

"Better looking than you, isn't she?" Big Thug said, laughing uproariously, pushing Prue in front of him as he left the hut.

Entering further into the gloom of the hut, it took my eyes a few seconds to adjust to the darkness.

"Phibah ... I'm back ... Phibah ..."

As I knelt beside her, I could tell that her fever had worsened, and Phibah was in a very bad way. She looked like she didn't have long to live. I wet her parched lips, but she was too weak to drink. I used a cloth and the cool water to swab her arms and her forehead. While sponging her down, I told her stories and sang her some old, old songs. Slowly but surely, I managed to calm her down and relax. It felt good to be able to ease some of her pain.

"Give my love to Masego," Phibah whispered.

"I will."

"And tell him I'm sorry that I was gone so long ..."

"I will."

I nearly died when the hut door was pushed open and I saw another of the Big Thugs standing there.

"What the hell are you doing here?" he roared at me.

"Phibah is very sick."

"Stand up when you talk to me!"

I quickly jumped to my feet.

"Phibah's very sick, sir. She's burning up with fever!"

"What are you blathering on about, girl? Why are you wasting your time with a thing like this?"

"Her condition is getting worse, sir, much worse."

"I don't have time to waste on some stupid slave like this. I have far too much to do today. I'll staunch her pain for her, you wait and see." He produced his whip from his boot and lashed Phibah two or three times.

"Don't!" I shouted, without thinking. The Big Thug stopped and grabbed me violently by the throat.

"What did you say, bitch?"

I apologised over and over again but he ignored me and tightened his grip on my throat so that I couldn't breathe. He wasn't going to let me go before insulting me further. Raising my dress, he raped me there and then.

"Go back to the fields, you dirty cow," he said between gritted teeth.

"If I see you around here again wasting your work-time on this old bag of bones, I'll beat you so badly nobody will be able to recognise you."

One of the hardest things I have had to do in my life was to walk out of that hut as that thug stared me down, and leave Phibah to her fate.

THE REALISATION

I'm trying to immerse myself in warm and soothing thoughts today, my mind hungry for consolation and calm. I'm remembering Mum hugging me and my dear Dad swinging me around in circles as I laughed loudly. I'm thinking about home and remembering that hour before bed when Mum would sing me a song before giving me a goodnight kiss, and holding me tight.

When I think back and remember those times, I remind myself that there's still love in this world, and that everywhere isn't like here. I think of the good people I've known down through the years, and generous people around me here who would share their last piece of bread with you. Despite the brutality we witness regularly, we who work as slaves do our best to be kind and to help one another whenever we can.

Working in the fields today, I watched as Fortune did his best to keep up with the rest of us who are much older and stronger than him. Fortune is still just a little boy and yet he's so determined. I feel very protective towards him even if he's always trying to act older than he is. When I tried to give him a hug today, he moved away from me. He probably thinks that hugs and cuddles are just childish things now, even if he's still just six years old. Kids grow old and hard against the world so quickly in this place. And this is no surprise – only half of the kids born here survive into adulthood. They soon come to understand the life they've been born into. They realise that slavery awaits them in this world too and little else, that it's been written on their skin. As a result, they tiptoe out of it as quick as they can. It's as if these babies have sensed that a sweeter path exists and leave this Earth no sooner than they've entered it, that it's better for them to try their luck in the next world.

It can't be any worse than this one.

There are other times when Fortune is ready to have a hug and needs someone to cuddle up next to. And when I sit outside the hut some nights, alone with my thoughts before sleeping, Fortune will appear and sit beside me and he'll let me hug him close. There are times when he'll put his hand in mine and we'll sit there quietly for a long time – unless someone else comes along, that is! Then he quickly moves away and goes back acting all grown-up again.

I can't stop thinking about poor Phibah today, now that she's started her journey to the next world. I hope and pray that she'll take good care of the souls of all the lost children. I try to imagine what her journey will be like. The journey between sadness and joy, between suffering and peace, between this world and the next.

Phibah's journey will be nothing like our journey on The Nightmare, from our homes to this place on the other side of the earth.

And it hits me then that we're here for good and that we can never go home, and I'm filled with despair.

We have so many stories and songs about exile and the return but we'll never go back. We try and convince ourselves that one day we'll return to the Land of Memories but this is just a mirage or a dream. How could we ever return home? Even if we did manage to escape from here, where would we get a ship to make the journey? It's only the slavemasters who own ships. This is the reality of it. The truth is that simple. I will never return home. I will never see Dad and Mum and Nague ever again. This realisation sends a terrible shudder through my body. The people we once knew all belong to our past now. I have no more hope of seeing Dad and Mum alive on this Earth again than poor Phibah has of seeing me. We're in different worlds.

And the only reason we sing the songs and tell the tales of return is because the idea of being lost so far away forever is too terrible to bear thinking about.

THE PAINTER

I was cutting the cane as usual the other day when I saw something that astonished me. A man stood at the side of the field staring at us. He was a white man, but he wasn't was an overseer or slavemaster and there was nothing threatening about him. He wore a big wide-brimmed hat for shade from the sun and when he noticed us staring at him, he lowered his head immediately. He had a wooden stand in front of him with pots of different colours, and a pencil in his hand. He was marking something that we couldn't see on a flat piece of wood. Was he counting us in case someone had escaped?

"Have you noticed that man?" I asked Anna.

"Yes, he's doing something with a pencil."

"Hopefully he's not up to something bad ..."

The man moved his position more than once and bent his head to the wooden stand and began marking something again. Fortune ran over to tell us what was going on.

"He's drawing a picture," he said excitedly, "in different colours!"

This was interesting.

"How do you know?"

"I sneeked up behind him to see."

"Fortune! You could have been whipped for doing it! What did you see?"

"He has a brush and paint and he's painted the field and everyone working in it. The picture looked lovely."

For the rest of that afternoon I wondered to myself why the Man in the Hat was doing such a thing. It was strange. He was making an image of us and putting it on canvas. Why? That was the question. Phibah and Lydia had told us that there are many pictures on the walls of the Big House. Some are pictures of people and some are pictures of places.

But who in the world would want to take pictures of us? And Fortune says that this place looks nice in the Man's picture.

I straightened my back and glanced around me. How could he possibly think of this plantation as a nice place? If we'd been able to sit down and rest and have enough food in our mouths we might have thought of this place differently. If we hadn't been separated from our families forever. If we'd something to looking forward to. If they hadn't whipped and killed so many of us, we wouldn't be so full of bitterness and hate. If only we had some control over our own time, maybe we'd view this place differently? If …If … No! There's no way that this man could ever make a good picture, or something that was real or true. Surely, no one would would want to put his picture on the wall of their home?

I looked around me again. The Man with the Hat was gone.

,

A NEW LIFE

A new life came into our midst this evening. Dinah gave birth to a daughter, and they are both healthy. I went to see the new baby early in this morning before work – she looks so small and perfect. Her name is Dido. But the Overseer will give her another name and this will be hers as soon as she's able to work, and that's how she'll be known "officially" from now on.

Looking at her, I was filled with awe. I was amazed at how small and perfect her fingers and toes were. The way she kept her little eyes closed. How strange and wonderful it is that she'd been in the womb just a few hours earlier and for a full nine months, and here she is now with us in this world! It's truly a miracle. I fell instantly in love with her. And it struck me suddenly – this is what Mum must have felt, too, when I was born. Just as Dinah can't stop staring at this beautiful little miracle of hers, it was the same for my mum. And Hagar must have held me with her tiny fingers the way Dido clings to Dinah's hand also. Thinking such thoughts made me sad and I pushed such images to the back of my mind.

I imagined what it would be like if I was in Dinah's position, if I was a mother too. It's not impossible that this would happen some day. How would it feel to have a baby, I wonder? At first, I'd probably feel afraid. Afraid of the responsibility for a new life such as little Dido. I'd have to look after and feed and raise a small, vulnerable little human being that was half me! But then if I had someone to give me a helping hand, maybe things would be fine. Maybe I could do it then and have a baby some day too? And I'd never be completely lonely in the world then, as I'd always have someone else for company. We'd grow up together, and I'd raise my little baby and give her all my love – I'd give her everything that I had. The thought of loving someone else so much …

But then, what about the sadness when they took the child from me, to be sold as a slave to someone else? I had to consider this awful reality too. There's nothing sadder than having your children taken away from you. And this has happened to so women that I know. It's one thing to be stolen from your family by others who claim that they own you, and that you don't have any rights from then on. But it's another thing again for them to steal the fruit of your womb, your own flesh and blood and then to sell your child for profit. This is the lowest and most disgusting thing any human beings can do. They've stolen your family and your birthright not once but twice! And every day for the rest of your life, you'll feel that terrible grief and loss, and suffer every new morning.

Dido has just woken up from sleep. She's opened her eyes.

QUASHA

Every so often the Overseer rings a bell and announces that it's Sunday. The day they call "Sunday" comes around regularly, and the white men here on the plantation consider it a special day. They go into a church where they worship, and there's a separate hut which we're told to go into. The man who preaches to us is always a white man, but none of the slavemasters, or the Overseer, are in the congregation. On Sundays, we don't go to the fields, but work at home on small patches of land or gardens where we weed and hoe. It's tiring, but not as tiring as working in the big fields cutting the cane.

Quasha came over to me last Sunday and handed me a bowl of peas.

"Why are you giving me these, Quasha?"

"I have too many of them myself."

I knew this was just a fib and I gave him a sceptical look.

"Why are you being so nice to me again today?"

"Again?"

It felt a bit silly by now.

"Ebony ... Tell me what I can do to make you happy ..."

"You can help me do a bit of weeding here if you want to know the truth," I say.

And this was exactly what we did – Quasha and me working together! And while we were weeding, we had a good chat and it was a lovely way to pass the time. I was so relaxed and comfortable with Quasha, I didn't notice the time passing. We understand one another. And it just feels so good and natural when someone can be there beside you, keeping you company. The small boss is on duty on Sundays and he's a much quieter man. He's not as rough as the others and you don't need to look over your shoulder all the time. Things are quieter. And my stomach wasn't in knots with the fear of him. Oh, how good it would be to have these calm feelings every day!

IMAGES RETURNING TO MY MIND

They keep coming back to me at the most unexpected times. Images of the journey we made to this place on The Nightmare, images and memories I thought long gone. Although I try to wipe them from my mind, they return and make themselves real again. I shut my eyes tightly and try to push the images away, but they're stronger than me. The more I fight them, the stronger they become. And because we're not allowed to talk while working, each of us is isolated in our lonely island of remembering, and the rough waves come back and pound the shore, waves so fierce that they overcome me. And yet Hagar is there beside me, even in the midst of the darkest memories of all. I want to see her and feel her presence again, but not like this.

I'm lying on my back, at the bottom of The Nightmare, rising and falling, rising and falling with every pitch and surge of the waves. The ship is rocking and I sway from side to side, as if to the rhythm of cutting the cane at work. I grab hold of Hagar's dress, the yellow dress with the black circles on it, so that we don't roll away from one another on the timber and it makes me feel safe.

I'm back there now again in my mind, in the worst hell, with all the screams and moans of pain and fear. None of us know where we are or why this is happening to us. All we know is that our lives as we knew them are over – this is the horror that torments our heart and soul.

WASHING

Belinda and I were put in the same cabin after Phibah died, and Clara and Anna joined us. This is a sign that we're getting older, that we've nearly reached adulthood. It's nicer to be in a cabin than in a room full of women, and it's quieter here too. And when we come in from the fields at sundown, we have an opportunity to wash our clothes in privacy and hang them behind the house to dry. Talo watches us from the back of her cabin.

"You're lucky – you still have the strength left to wash clothes after all the work today," she says smiling.

I ask if she'd like me to wash clothes some clothes for her but she refuses. Talo is a fiercely proud and independent woman.

Unless I'm so exhausted that I can barely stand, I don't mind the job of washing clothes and Belinda's company helps. I like the feel of the cool water on my arms, it soothes the scratches and cuts I've suffered during the day. The flannel skirt is heavy and takes a long time to dry out, but the other clothes are lighter and easier to wash and dry. I notice some tears in my clothes where the threads have come loose. Once washed, we hang the clothes on the line outside and sing together in low voices. The clothes come alive as they flutter in the wind. I stand there for a while and watch them dancing in the breeze, dancing as if they were free.

STORY

Last night, I repaired the hole in my skirt, but the flannel has become so fragile it's difficult to hold it together. It's worn beyond repair and no matter how much I try pulling the threads together, it's useless. I'll just have to keep an eye out for a spare piece of cloth and sew a patch onto the skirt at some stage. It'll be a long time yet before we get a chance to make any new clothes.

Not that this is important tonight, because I'm listening to Anna tell the children a story about Anasi spinning a web to reach the sun. The children – and Fortune is amongst them – are crowded around and listening on in wonder. Quasha sits down next to me.

"I was watching you when you were out washing the clothes," he says.

"This needs concentrating on ... it ravels in front of my very eyes ... but it's nice to listen to a the story about the magic web the gods wove while mending."

"This is a totally different place at night time, isn't it, Ebony?"

I raise my head and look around at the children enjoying the story, and the older people tending to their gardens and their animals outdoors. If Big Vulture was around, we wouldn't be able to relax in one another's company, or feel at peace.

I glance over at Fortune.

"What are you thinking about?" asks Quasha.

"Fortune – he has a distant look in his eyes. I know he's thinking of the time he witnessed his mother being whipped."

"And how is she now?" asks Quasha in a hesitant voice.

"She didn't survive the attack," I whisper.

I notice Quasha grimace and the way his fists go rigid.

"What are we doing here, Ebony? We're just fooling ourselves here telling each other stories as if it was still the good old days! This is just stupid and ridiculous, isn't it?"

I glance at his face and see the passion in his eyes.

"But what should we do?"

"Rebel. We need to rise up against our masters and take the fight to them, it's as simple as that."

"That's scary talk," I say angrily. "Do you want to find yourself hanging from a tree and your dead body being fed to the wild animals?"

Quasha says nothing and remains quiet for a long time afterwards, but I could feel his rage burning in the darkness.

A SERVICE

I don't think that Big Vulture and his friends have an understanding of spiritual matters or religious beliefs at all. They claim that our beliefs are superstitious and dangerous, and want us to believe the same things as them. Everything that we believe is important to our lives they consider to be both foolish and wrong. They think that everything they believe is both right and good. But the opposite is the case. They've got everything back to front; it is they who are wrong.

All that matters to them is law and order, and a multitude of rules. They love control and power so much, as well as proclaiming and enforcing rules. And every Sabbath, they read from a big book and claim that their rules are listed in it, rules that we should obey. We've heard this from the white men so many times. We're here to serve but especially to obey ... to obey ... to obey. The white men claim that it's written in their Big Book – that the black people are deemed to be slaves, and that it's their role since the beginning of time to serve the whites. We don't understand where they get these ideas.

We have no book that lays down rules which we've invented ourselves. We don't preach that the black people are better than others, that we're good and that others are less worthy than us. We don't have any book at all. We live in harmony with the natural world and treat the Earth just as our forefathers did. We were given a piece of land to live on and animals to look after, and the Earth provides us with sustenance and food, just as it does rain and sun. And the world and its peoples were at peace then.

We don't believe that any Great Book exists that claims people have to be robbed of their lands, have chains put around their necks, whipped, broken and cursed for the rest of their lives – and their children and their children's children? This is evil, pure evil and it should never be preached under the guise of any religion.

And yet we're forced to go to these services organised by the white men and listen to these strange interpretations of humankind. I never had feeling of hate before this, and yet, what I have experienced here makes me full of hate. Hatred is like a disease that spreads from one man to another.

THE MARK

Every time I wash, I'm aware of the mark on my shoulder where they branded me a slave. I've never seen it properly but I know that it's there. I wasn't born with this scar but was marked with it when we were brought to this place. It's on my left shoulder, and will be there forever. It's more than a scar – it means I'm marked for life.

Every time I touch the damaged skin there I'm reminded that I belong to someone else. I'm not an individual human being but someone else's property instead. And this is why I hate this scar.

This branding with the hot iron was one of the first things they did to us when we were taken off The Nightmare on arrival in the place they call the New World. The minute we were sold to the highest bidder we were branded. I still remember it as if it was yesterday. I can see them put the iron in the fire and then when it's red hot, it's set on the new slave's shoulder, whether man or woman. And I remember the smell most of all, a smell that none of us had experienced before. And the terrible agonised and frightened screaming – the way that each of us was held down by two and sometimes three people. I remember thinking, they won't do it to me because I'm still a child. But they made no distinction between us. They grabbed the woman in front of me, wrestled her to the ground and branded her. And then two men did the same to me.

I have never experienced such intense pain as that branding and the days that followed it. I thought I was going to die.

And in the minds of our tormentors we became adults that day, even if we ourselves remained as children. I couldn't understand why they did this to us on our arrival in this new country. It wasn't as if they could lose us or that we could ever escape them. We had no idea where we were – we didn't even know what country we were in. Now I realise that it was the white man known as Big Vulture who demanded that we be branded, to show that we belonged to him. This was the sole purpose of the mark – to demonstrate that we're their property, that we belonged to them. And to ensure that we never forget this for as long as we live. As if we could ever forget it ...

A NEW BEGINNING

Quasha and I are very close. He's like a breath of fresh air around the place whenever he calls in to chat. He's been in the plantation for as long as I can remember. Lately, we've become a lot closer. In the evenings, we sit and chat until well after the sun has gone down and he's been calling by with gifts for me.

The other night, he asked me whether I'd like to go for a walk with him down to the river, and I agreed. And it was really nice – just him and me – and the weight of the day's labour lightened as we spoke. He grabbed my hand, and I gave a giggle.

"What's so funny, Ebony?"

"This," I said, glancing at our entwined hands, "it's like you and me are boyfriend and girlfriend."

He didn't look embarrassed about it at all.

"Are you okay with that?"

I said I was, I nodded and gave a smile. Did I say I this because I like Quasha, or is it just that I feel rather grown up having a boyfriend? I'm getting to that age where I should be in love. We talked and talked for what seemed like hours and then Quasha fell silent for a long time.

"Can I ask you something?"

"Sure."

"What is your real name?

The slavemasters gave us all different names here, names that had nothing to do with us, that had no meaning, but Quasha wants to know my real name, my African name. So I told him.

"Yamba. Yamba is my name."

The minute I say it, the word sounds strange on my tongue. It's so long since I've spoken my own name. Because it was something private and it belonged to me.

"Would you like me to call you by this name?" Quasha asked.

For a moment, I wasn't sure.

"I never use it ... it was Mum and Dad's name for me and Hagar ... my sister. She was the last one I heard saying my real name."

"What happened to her?"

"Hagar died on the ship ... To tell you the truth, Quasha, I don't think of myself as Yamba anymore. Yamba was a free person. The name just doesn't sound right with me now ..."

Before that evening, I'd never tried to put words on these thoughts of mine. I'd pushed them to the back of my mind instead. Quasha put his arm around me.

"That's all right," he said, holding my hand.

"Thank you, Quasha."

Slowly, he turned towards mine and his lips were on mine. I shook my head.

"Ebony?"

"I don't want that, Quasha."

I could feel the electricity between us but I knew that I had to tread carefully and to take things slowly.

"But it's the most natural thing in the world, isn't it, it's like holding hands," he said, his hands still in mine.

"Hand holding is fine ... but that's all," I said firmly.

Quasha accepted this, and I loved him all the more for it, even if he didn't really understand.

I can't tell him about the awful things that the White Man did to me, the way he touched me and poked me and did what he wanted with my body.

WRITING

I wonder what writing feels like? I wonder what it would be like if I could write these thoughts down? Imagine if all these thoughts that I have – in the diary of my mind – could be put on paper. Imagine if they were something physical and real and on paper so that they could be remembered and saved for those who came after us. Imagine if our children's children and the generations of our blood that follow could read and re-read these thoughts and words of ours ... Surely, this would be a wonderful feeling.

Imagine if I myself could read – if, when I'm old, I could read something I wrote when I was young. What a wonderful thing! What a miracle! It must be like looking at a picture of a different time or place for as long as you want to, as long as you need to. The lines and layers of paint and the layers of meaning you discover every time you look at it.

Yet I can do this with my Memory, even if I can't record it in words or write anything down. Now that I'm older I can go back to my childhood, and remember the feelings I had at different times – love, sorrow, joy, pain. I haven't lived so many summers yet ... And still, I wonder what it's like to have the gift of writing, to record something of yourself with ink on the page ... I've seen some of the slavemaster's family reading in the garden and I'd love to be able to read.

I wouldn't waste time reading my own diary. Instead, I'd read other people's stories. It'd be like getting into other people's minds and trying to understanding their thoughts and feelings. I can't imagine such a thing, really. Does everyone feel the same as me, or would I read new thoughts and feelings in their minds, or discover new possibilities and ideas about the world?

THOUGHTS

What happens to someone's diary when they die? I never thought of this before. Do some people take their diaries with them to the grave, or destroy them before they pass on? I would never keep a record of my thoughts, in case someone else who could read would see them. They would be me my thoughts, and mine only.

There are things I'd never record. Things I want to forget but never can. They're in the corners of my Memory, moaning and gathering dust, but they're there – and I know that. They'll never fade or disappear.

The hundreds of eyes. That's one of my worst nightmares. When we came off The Nightmare, it was a terrible shock, something that I'll never forget.

SHAME

The feeling of continuous movement from the ship stopped and we were led on unsteady feet next to a timber platform which they'd set up in front of a building. We were lined up one after another, each of us chained together. It was strange to see the others properly after being below deck in darkness for weeks on end. Until then, we'd only known one another by our voices. We were all very frightened as we had no idea what was going to happen next. One after another, we were sent out onto this platform. There was so much shouting and noise, we were all petrified. They splashed water on us as if they were cleaning us, then made us wrap ourselves in sacks as a form of clothing.

The white men whom we discovered later were the slavetraders then pushed and pulled at us, and forced us to open our mouths; they fingered our hair and our bodies and even touched our private parts while talking amongst themselves. I was so scared at the sight of the whips in their hands, and the way they kept shouting at us in a strange language that we didn't understand. The rumour was that the White Man wanted to eat us.

In the end, I too was pushed onto the timber platform and made to stand on a box in full view of the white people. All those hundreds of eyes staring at me. I shut my eyes so that I couldn't see them, and the crowd laughed. I felt those hundreds of eyes burn right through me. Then there was silence, and I heard the crude voice of this one man shouting things at us, even if we had no idea what he was saying ... I thought he was cursing us. Later we realised that he was the merchant and that we were his produce. Like animals, we were for sale!

The memory of that multitude of eyes will never leave me. I've never felt so ashamed, even if I didn't understand what I'd done wrong. The feeling of those eyes staring me up and down from head to toe like a farm animal ... I hated all those insolent eyes, I wanted to tear them out of their skulls and squash each one. And then this man came out of the crowd and forced my mouth open and squeezed the skin on my arms and legs. Then another man appeared and did the same. And there was nowhere I could run to or hide. All I could do was stand there, completely humiliated, in my chains. When would the nightmare come to an end? Our hell didn't end but thankfully, no one ate us either.

A KISS

I let Quasha kiss me last night. It was one of the most important nights of my young life – it was as if I'd crossed an important threshold. I haven't told anyone our secret yet.

We'd gone for a walk by the river, and had sat in silence for a long time. We were so comfortable with one another by then, it was as if we could read one another's thoughts. There was no need for words. Quasha was gently stroking my hand when we looked at one another and began to kiss. It was completely natural with him – and Quasha is so tender and loving. I hugged him and he put his arm around me and as he kissed me gently on the nape of my neck, he then touched the skin on my shoulder and caressed the mark the branding iron had made. Suddenly, I felt ashamed, and pulled away.

"Ebony, what's wrong?"

"Don't touch that, it's an ugly part of my body."

"But it's not your fault."

Of course it's my fault, I said, but poor Quasha didn't understand. I've felt nothing but shame since I was taken from home and brought here as a slave. I've felt nothing but shame since they put that terrible mark on me. This brought tears to Quasha's eyes. He was desperate that I shouldn't feel this way. He tried to comfort me by saying that we were treated worse than animals and that this was no reflection on us. He also showed me his scar.

But his words made little sense to me in that moment. I've lived with the shame and the disgrace of it for so long that it's part of my very being. Ever since Hagar died, I have suffered this shame and guilt, my guilt entwined with my poor sister's death. It would be good not to feel such shame or guilt, or if only someone could wash it off me by some miracle. And because we were there together at the time, I associate the mark on my shoulder with the loss of Hagar. There's only so much insult or shame that someone can take before they collapse under the burden of it and accept it as if it was part of their very essence. This is why the kiss with Quasha was so sweet and pure tonight. The idea of someone accepting me as I was, and wanting to kiss me and show me love. What a precious feeling! I'll relive this in my memory over and over again.

PLAITING THE HAIR

After finishing our long day of work in the fields, we have many other tasks to complete before it's time for sleep. We prepare food, eat, wash and carry hay to the mules and other animals. Only after the last roll-call of the day are we free to go to sleep and by then we're usually exhausted.

Tonight, Belinda and I are in a good mood and she asks me to braid her hair before going to bed. I weave her tresses by candlelight, and I'm content. Outdoors, the night has gone quiet except for the sound of the animals grazing on the grass and hay and the occasional howl of a coyote in the distance.

"Just for one evening, let's imagine what it's like to wear clothes that are new and bright," says Belinda, "instead of the boring work clothes we have to wear every day."

"Anything would be better than this flannel," I say.

"Imagine what it must be like to wear fine clothes every day, like the people up in the Big House. Colourful clothes that are comfortable to wear. I'm sure that we would feel so much better in ourselves."

"Would you like a job up in the Big House, Belinda?" I said, laughing.

"My skin is a far too dark for that, they just wouldn't accept me there."

"I'm only joking, my dear," I said, imitating a posh

voice. "What I mean is I don't think you should be actually doing a job there at all, just living the high life. It'd be good to do nothing, just dressing up and going out for afternoon picnics in the pony and trap!"

We both laughed at such fanciful and crazy thoughts. I finished plaiting her hair, and Belinda wrapped her head in a cloth scarf. Then we both settled down in our make-shift beds on the floor beneath blankets, next to the fireplace.

"Thank you, Ebony. Hey! We see Quasha in your company all the time now. You're a real couple now, aren't you?"

"Yes, I suppose so. Quasha's a good man, a man who's worth his weight in gold."

"Good for you, that's all I can say. Good night, Ebony."

"Good night."

PRELUDE

I'm back in the fields again, myself and my knife hacking into the undergrowth and chopping the cane. It's very hot today and the work is monotonous and drags on. It's quite a while before we have breakfast. Already this morning, since the sound of the bell awakened us, we've been spreading manure and harvesting the cane. I feel happier than usual because my mind is on the future now rather than the past best. Prior to this, the future appeared before me as a great and unknown void, something I was afraid and anxious about, but I'm now beginning to feel differently. As Quasha and I have become closer, something very much like hope is forming in me, and it's a strange and wonderful feeling. Instead of thinking the worst about my life ahead, I sense that a different path may lie ahead for me. If things continue like this, and Quasha and I form an enduring relationship, then maybe we'll be blessed with a child, and I'll have a family that I can call my own again. I know that we'll never be able to return home – back to the Land of Memories again – but at least I won't be alone in this world. Quasha understands how I feel. My closeness to him is the nearest thing to what I had with Hagar once. He's someone whom I can share all of my worries and fears with, and the joyful times that still might be ours. He's a great friend, and this is a lovely, warm feeling to have in your life. Maybe this is a prelude to a better life.

CLEANING THE WOUNDS

"Ebony !! Ebony!!" the screams rang out.

I rushed outside to where Fortune was shouting loudly in a petrified voice.

"Ebony, come quickly!"

Fortune ran off in the direction of the Big House and I followed him to where a crowd had formed a circle on the green opposite the Big House. Someone was being whipped. Who were the slavemasters punishing this time?

I squeezed through between the watchers and gave a gasp of despair on seeing Belinda on the floor. Half her shirt was torn away, and Big Thug was whipping her mercilessly. Belinda had her arms above her head in an effort to protect herself but her back was in ribbons and her blood had mixed into the dust. My legs gave way beneath me and I felt myself collapsing with the shock. Two people grabbed hold of me and stopped me from striking the ground too hard. I passed out. When I came to myself, most of the crowd had disappeared except for one or two people who stood looking down at Belinda. Groggily, I got to my feet and went over to her.

"I'm here, Belinda," I said, holding her hand. "Are you able to make it home?" I whispered to her.

"I can't move for the moment," Belinda said weakly.

"We'll bring her home," said the others. "Go and prepare things."

They carried her back to the cabin. I was like someone in a dream, placing cool water in a bowl and adding some herbs to the mixture. They laid Belinda gently on the floor and I washed her painful wounds.

I surprised myself with my lack of tears. I was amazed at how resilient she was – how few tears she shed. I dabbed at the terrible lacerations the whip had made all along her torn back. Beautiful Belinda, so sweet and kind ... her skin had been marked for life. How long did they seek to leave their mark on us, on our very skin and bone? And Belinda was just one victim amongst many hundreds of them. I had applied this balm to the wounds before, and would do so again. There was nothing to stop these tyrants. This abuse might continue for hundreds of years – the same as before. It was just our turn now.

Would it be our children's turn in the years to come?

REBELLION

I couldn't meet Quasha last night as we'd previously
arranged because Belinda had been hurt so badly. I was
desperate to meet him the following night, however.
Quasha is so kind. The first thing he did was to see if I
was alright, but I could barely communicate with him, I
was still so traumatised after what'd happened to poor
Belinda. I could see that Quasha was in a hurry to share
some news with me. Looking into his eyes, I could tell
that he was all fired up.

"There's going to be a protest," he said, searching my
face for a response.

"Make sure not to be involved, Quasha," I said, in
warning. "If something happens to you, after what
they've just done to Belinda, I'll lose my mind
completely."

Quasha shook his head.

"No, it's nothing like that, I can assure you. This is
completely different. This doesn't involve any violence or
fighting … It's the simplest plan in the world to be
honest, and I want to be a part of it." He smiled, and put
his hands on my shoulders. "All we have to do is stop
working. After two more sunsets – the date has been
fixed – we're going to refuse to go into the fields the
following morning. We'll down tools and everyone will
refuse to work for Big Thug. No one will do the
blacksmith's work, none of us will gather the canes into

the warehouses, no one will cut and winnow the sugar canes, no one ..."

I have to be honest and admit that his words made no sense to me.

"But they'll punish us, won't they, Quasha?"

"Wait ... I'm not finished! We'll all agree to return to work right away, but only on one condition – that they pay us for our labour."

"Pay us? Don't be silly, they'll never ..."

Quasha stared at me and I could see in his face that he was agitated.

"This protest is organised on a huge scale, Ebony. There are some ten thousand of us downing tools at the same time. They won't know what to do about it! If we're all united and refuse to do the work, then they're in big trouble. All production will come to a halt. They can whip us and beat us all they want, but it'll make no difference! Without us, the workers, there's nothing ... there's no sugar trade ... there's nothing!"

"They'll think of something."

Quasha rose to his feet and paced around the room.

"It's up to them! It's in their hands! They're rotten with money! If they begin to pay us for our labour for the first time, the whole show will be up and running again! We can pressure them to change. The lure of profit and money will be too much for them!"

"But Quasha, the whole point of slavery is that you work for nothing ..."

Quasha hestitated.

"Yes, but once they pay us ..."

We both said the words at the same time, "... we'll no longer be in bondage!"

We both laughed at the madness of the idea, but Quasha carried on.

"We'll continue as before, but everything will be different – everything will be new. From now on, we'll have rights ... we can bargain with them as regards our sweat and labour. It's going to change everything!" His enthusiasm for the plan was overwhelming.

But it was Belinda's scars and the image of her back torn to ribbons that filled my mind, and this, mixed with anger and anxiety, curbed me from sharing Quasha's excitement.

"You wait and see. They'll have another way out of this. They always do. They always think of something to beat us ..."

Quasha gave a heavy sigh.

"I know. I understand what you mean. But this plan's worth trying. Some missionary on one of the plantations on the other side, a good distance from here, came up with this plan and he's been working on it for many months. Thousands of us have agreed to take part in this revolt with him, and I have a good feeling that this will work!"

Quasha couldn't stay long tonight. He kissed me with one long fierce kiss and then he was gone. I watched him disappear into the fading dusk.

I never saw him again.

CHANCE

How many chances is one person given in this life? How many chances to change things? This was what I was thinking as I considered what to do. How much worse could life be if I made a break for it with the others? How many times did I want to suffer the shame of being whipped, raped and left bereaved? How many more times did I want to witness others being tortured and punished to within an inch of their lives, to have to cleanse and heal the wounds suffered by my friends? I wanted this horror to end soon. Quasha's love meant everything to me and he wanted to risk everything with this mad plan of escape ... this crazy break for freedom.

But was it worth the try? Could I live with myself if I didn't take the chance? I really wanted to seize the moment, though I couldn't even imagine what a different life would be like. We were together, Quasha and I, and this was enough. The secret plan of escape went from one cabin to another in whispers. Two sunsets ... and this was it. One sunset after this evening's.

THE LAST DAY

This was one of the best days of my life – one of the best days since I first came into this world. I felt like a different person all day long. I woke up feeling excited, as everything in the world seemed new. I even saw the pigs through new eyes when I went out to feed them ... the dawn that broke across the sky was fresh and promising. Now I had something to live for, and this powerful new energy filled the world with a new wonder. It was in the sky above each of us and flowing through us like a great secret. Is this how other people live, with a real purpose to their lives, with something to look forward to?

I even sliced the cane with a strength that I hadn't had before, muttering aloud to myself, "This is the last time I do this as as slave! Next time, I'll do this work for payment – my labour will be undertaken for a fair price." And each time the old doubts appeared in my mind, I refused to give them space. I wanted this one day – one single day of my life – where I could focus entirely on the good things that I prayed were to come.

One more sunset, and that new day of hope would dawn. Hope would become a reality.

THE EMBERS AND THE FLAME

We misinterpreted the flames that shot up into the sky.

We heard the shouts outside and ran out to see the fire climbing high. We jumped up and down, we shouted and sang of freedom. It was a still, dark night. Everyone fell silent, staring at the flames as if we found it difficult to believe that they were real at all. It's really happened! The day has finally come around! But the day had not dawned ... tomorrow had not come.

The hut where we dried out the canes was on fire. Then we started talking among ourselves. Was the fire part of the plan of escape? At first we weren't sure. It seemed too early to be sure of anything ... all we knew was that it was morning ... But it had started now, too early ... the revolt was underway. There was no turning back now! This was it. The chanting, the shouting, the singing, the dancing... The men ran outside and the fire was spreading. The crackling of plant and cane ... all across the fields ... the crops were cracking apart as if they were protesting against the heat.

This was the moment! The fields were aflame. All the fields where we'd sweated out our lives year on year, where we'd sweated blood ... they were finally burning up. The misery and suffering was at an end. Tomorrow, we won't have to down our tools and refuse to work in the fields – there won't be any fields left! Tomorrow would bring the final rebellion when we refused to work in the fields that were burned to cinders. We heard gunfire as the loud shots rang out but it made no difference to us. All the rules were gone now, they meant nothing. Fire and flame! The drums sounding out! The shouts and the cries of freedom! It was there in everyone's face, that mixture of fear and celebration. What's happening? Nobody is too sure, it's a mix of chaos and confusion but we know our day of deliverance is near.

Our feet strike out across the dry ground ... everyone is running to the internal rhythm of our hearts ... the sound of freedom. In every direction we look, there are more and more flames rising into the night sky. We've never seen anything like it. This is it, the moment of our lives!

Click! Bang! A gunshot rang out!

Next come the pounding sounds of horses' hooves and I was completely confused. This wasn't part of the plan, was it? The slavemasters come galloping through the flames to pursue us and we scatter in all directions.

The familiar click, click of guns and bullets. Have our hopes been raised only to be dashed again so cruelly? Will this be the same as every other time when our revolt is put down and our hopes and dreams are destroyed? How many of them are there? Oh my God! And they're shooting at us – firing blindly into the darkness!

We were thrown in the air, and our world turned upside-down. We're so close and yet ... are our hopes to be raised again only for our world to be turned on its head?

The beat of the drum stops.

    The singing turns to confusion and screams.

      The crowd disperses and there is just confusion.

Bodies fall onto the dry earth,

    the horses rear up with fear ...

      The heat of the fires are getting closer as smoke
        fills the air.

The White Men are smashing our fragile huts to pieces, galloping over and through the fragile walls of straw, cooking pots smashed to pieces, dogs barking, chickens flying and the pigs running crazy and wild. I see glimpses between the shooting flames and the depths of darkness – Big Brute with his whip and gun, people running here, there and everywhere with terror in their eyes. Here ... there ... way across the fields ... there's nowhere to go ... death and danger lie everywhere. I hunker down and hide behind one of the huts and try to think of an escape. And between the stars and the flame, I glimpse Fortune and that knife that's far too big for him. Everyone scatters in all directions, running for their lives. I give a terrible scream.

    "Fortune !!!!"

My cry is in vain. Little Fortune is gunned down, his frail body falling as if in slow motion to the earth.

    My heart is filled with grief ...

    I take to my heels and run.

RUN

Running, running like the wind, her legs fast and strong, running to God knows where, slower then faster again, her body leaning forward into the wind, feeling the freedom. Who cares where? Just running as far away as possible, escaping that crazy hell.

Run, Ebony, run ... she's fleeing in terror but she doesn't care anymore ... her body could break into a thousand pieces and be scattered to the four winds.

She doesn't care anymore because she's lost everything now ... everything's gone. Any small hints of happiness slipped through her fingers long ago. They've long since disappeared.

Barefoot, her graceful fifteen-year-old body moves to a rhythm all of its own, across the plantation fields, her soles striking stones and hard ground. She feels the blood pumping through her, coursing through her, body and soul. The stink of smoke on the air makes breathing difficult. But there's nothing else. Run, Ebony, run for your life. Just the traces of your feet left behind on the rough dry soil. Traces that soon disappear ... traces of her passing.

As with her memory of what came before, this too is the best thing that can happen, because the less Ebony remembers of her young life, the better by far ...

She keeps on running, and she'll keep on running until the end of time, because she's still being persecuted.

When we leaf through the history books, there's no record of her. There's nowhere that offers her refuge or sanctuary. It's as if she never existed.

If only she could find sanctuary, a safe haven she could call home.

Keep running, don't stop, no matter what. Run, Yamba, run.

THE SORROWS OF YAMBA
(selection from the songs of a black slave girl)

Cease, ye British sons of murder!
Cease from forging Afric's chain;
Mock your Saviour's name no further,
Cease your savage lust of gain.

Ye that boast "Ye rule the waves",
Bid no slave ship soil the sea,
Ye that "never will be slaves",
Bid poor Afric's land be free.

Where ye gave to war its birth,
Where your traders fix'd their den,
There go publish "Peace on Earth",
Go proclaim "good-will to men".

Where ye once have carried slaughter,
Vice, and Slavery, and Sin;
Seiz'd on Husband, Wife, and Daughter,
Let the Gospel enter in.

'The Sorrows of Yamba' was published by Hannah More in 1797
and then later attributed to Eaglesfield Smith
as a co-author of the poem.

AFTERWORD

The inspiration to write this novel was the memorable exhibition by Welsh writer Manon Steffan Ros at Penrhyn Castle, Bangor, north Wales, in 2018. Her brief was to organize an exhibition on the link between the Penrhyn Estate and the slave trade. The exhibition made a lasting impression on me, and I began to write a novel about Lord Penrhyn (Richard Pennant). Then in March 2019, I heard a talk at the Slate Museum in Llanberis on the connection between the Welsh woollen trade and slavery.

The extent of the slave trade is so enormous that it's difficult for us to get a proper sense of it. By 1860, twelve million people had been taken from Africa as slaves (and nearly two thousand had died en route on the slave ships). As this trade grew during the 18th century, the enslaved people needed to be clothed. 'Welsh flannel', or 'Negro wool' as it was called, answered this demand. Weavers in the county of Meirionnydd and in mid-Wales wove coarse flannel for those who had been enslaved. According to Chris Evans, author of *Slave Wales*, one observer in the 1770s had noted that the Welsh woollens were "covering the poor Negroes in the West Indies". I hadn't known this story prior to this. One of my ancestors ran a fulling mill in Trawsfynydd, Meirionnydd, and it's quite possible that he would have been part of this trade.

In the end, I decided to explore the narratives of two young girls: Dorcas, who comes from a weaving community in Dolgellau, Meirionnydd, and who has to find employment as a

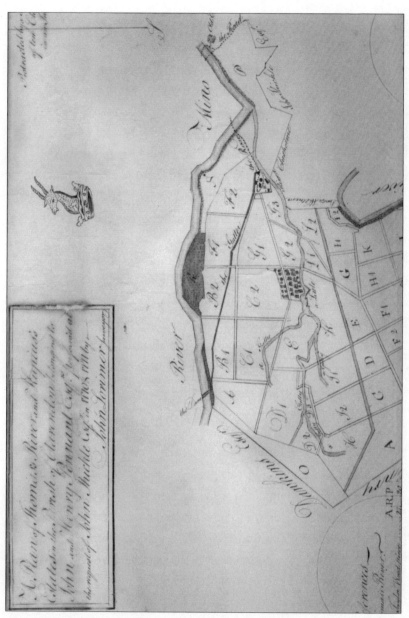

Some of the lands owned by the Pennant family in Clarendon, Jamaica, 1770

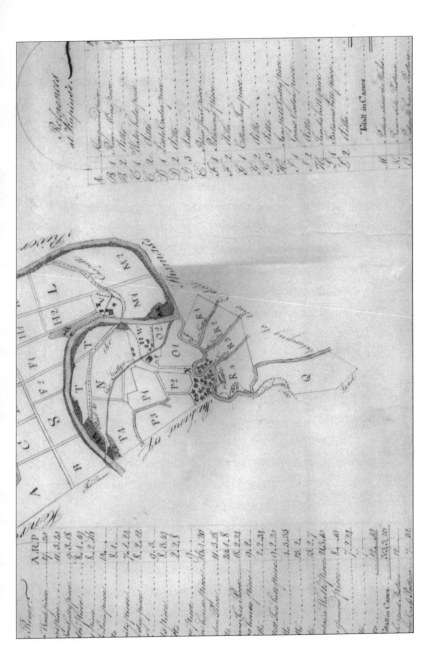

267

maid in Penrhyn Castle when the flannel market declines; and Ebony, a slave-girl in Jamaica, working on the Pennant Estates, the land of Lord Penrhyn. The only thing that the two female characters have in common is that they are both victims of Lord Penrhyn's pure greed for profit, something which has disastrous consequences for both of their lives. Lord Penrhyn (George Hay Dawkins-Pennant) doesn't appear in the novel, but his shadow looms ominously over the lives of both girls. The first part of the narrative encompasses Dorcas' story while the second half of the novel – Ebony's story – is set a few years earlier.

The huge wealth of the Penrhyn family was well known. Gifford Pennant came from Flintshire and he bought vast tracts of land in Jamaica. He was no small-time landowner – his estate was twenty times the size of most other estates at the time. Edward, his son (who died in 1736), became the Chief Justice of Jamaica. One of Edward's sons, John, increased the family fortune further through marriage, and ensured the acquistion of even more land in Jamaica. John returned to live in Britain; indeed, his son, Richard Pennant, 1st Baron Penrhyn (1737–1808), was born en-route during that sea journey

From then onwards, the family supervised the plantations from afar, through letters and overseers.

As well as managing the Jamaican estate, Richard Pennant was also a Member of Parliament for Liverpool, a city that was central to 90% of Britain's slave trade. He himself had a million slaves in Jamaica and was the chairman of the West Indian Committee. When William Wilberforce began his campaign to end slavery in 1788, Pennant campaigned energetically against abolition.

When the Slavery Abolition Act was passed in 1833, Lord Penrhyn was awarded £14,683 (the equivalent of £1.3 million today) in compensation for his loss. He was one of 46,000 British citizens who owned slaves. Millions of pounds were awarded in compensation at the time, and it's no surprise that the British Government didn't finish paying off these large sums of money until 2015. The enslaved people themselves never saw a penny of this profit.

The cost of building Penrhyn Castle today would be around £50,000,000, and it was slave money that paid for the bulk of this outrageous wealth. To discover the names of the enslaved, I searched the Penrhyn Estate archives in Bangor. As Dr John Llywelyn Williams noted, the legacy of slavery is still evident in the Dyffryn Ogwen area near Bangor. For example, strips of land similar to those tilled in Jamaica were used by Richard Pennant on 100 acres of Llandygái Mountain to grow potatoes in 1798. This wasn't due to Pennant's generosity. At a time of great hardship Pennant used the labour of unemployed quarrymen, whose families were suffering badly with hunger, to work the land and grow the crops for food there.

I knew a good deal about the Penrhyn Quarry Strike of 1900–03, the longest industrial dispute in British history, but I'd never heard the facts of Pennant's connection with slavery. It's this untold story that I've explored in this novel. The suffering experienced by slaves on the plantations makes for difficult reading when re-imagined in the form of fiction. The worst examples of what awaited African people after their journey to the West Indies have been recorded factually in the diary of Thomas Thistlewood. As Wilberforce said, "So much misery condensed in so little room is more than the human imagination had ever before conceived."

With regard to some of the furnishings and artefacts Dorcas saw in Penrhyn Castle as associated with Jamaica, I used the paintings of the plantations as a guide. These belong to a slightly later period, but I took the liberty of relocating them to the years around 1830. George Hay Dawkins-Pennant, the successor to Richard Pennant, is the Lord Penrhyn of the novel, the man who built the structure that is Penrhyn Castle as it stands today.

Ebony's story belongs to a slightly earlier time frame but, despite this, I refer to an uprising that resembles the Sam Sharpe Revolt of 1831 towards the end of my novel. Sharpe was a deacon with the Baptists, and it was his idea to organise a strike during the Christmas period. The night before the strike, a section of the Kensington Estate in Jamaica was set on fire. By midnight, there were fires in 16 other surrounding estates. There was a ferocious backlash on the part of the owners, and everyone who appeared before the courts following the rebellion was found guilty. It's estimated that 312 enslaved people were hanged in reprisal, and a thousand people were killed by the soldiers during the revolt itself. By May 1832, Sam Sharpe himself had also been executed. It's believed that the severity of this terrible atrocity – the revenge on the part of the slave-owners and authorities – made people aware of this scandalous regime and ensured that slavery was eventually abolished.

The enslaved people in the novel had to go to a specific church for black people organised by the estate, even if missionary work was being undertaken by Nonconformists such as Sam Sharpe at this time. The preaching of the message that all people were equal in the sight of God struck a chord with the abolitionists and helped to change longheld attitudes in this regard. A number of missionary leaders from this time came from the black community itself.

Religion plays a role in Dorcas' story too, as this is set in a period where many Welsh people rejected the State Church and became Nonconformists. Dorcas' family are Methodists from the Meirionnydd area, however her cousin's family (Cadi) are Church members. There was only a handful of Welsh people employed by the Penrhyn Estate in Bangor – it appears that Lord Penrhyn didn't trust them, and in the lists of servants, it's unusual to find a Welsh name. Cadi's family, therefore, would have had to be Church people in order to be employed in Penrhyn Castle.

At the time of writing this novel in autumn 2020, the vicious murder of George Floyd had happened in May, leading to protests world wide. The Black Lives Matter campaign has led many people to re-engage with the dreadful slave-trade era in history and its poisonous legacy which continues to affect mankind to this very day. While researching the history of this period over the past two years or so, I found it difficult to believe how cruel many white people were towards the black community at this juncture. And on viewing the infamous film footage of Derek Chauvin kneeling on George Floyd's neck for a full 9 minutes, I asked myself: "How can any one human being behave in this way towards another one of his fellow men?" The answer is because they can. The system still allows such atrocities to happen. It's allowed because the disgusting virus that is racism isn't challenged enough in society, and because anti-racism is not being taught in schools.

As a white person, I'm fully aware that I might not be the first choice to write about slavery, and I acknowledge this, but I have attempted to write about it, and hope that many others will do so in the future. Racism runs deep in our society, and the first step is to recognise this. If this novel will be a way of starting a discussion about racism, it will have achieved something.

Angharad Tomos
October 2020

"I'm not sad. I'm not sorry. I'm angry and I'm tired. I stopped crying years ago. I'm numb. I don't want your pity. I want change."

Letetra Widman, the sister of Jacob Blake,
who was shot in the back by a police officer, August 2020

Novels steeped in history

Exciting stories based on key historical events

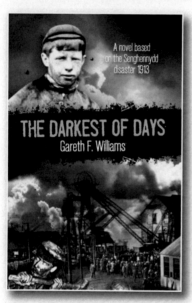

Winner of the 2014 Tir na-nOg award in the original Welsh

THE DARKEST OF DAYS
Gareth F. Williams

A novel based on the Senghennydd disaster 1913

£5.99

Shortly before 8.30 on the morning of 14 October 1913, 439 men and boys perished in a horrific explosion at Senghennydd coal mine.

John Williams was only eight years old when he and his family came from one of the slate mining villages of the north to live in Senghennydd, in the South Wales valleys. He looked forward to his thirteenth birthday, when he too would commence work in the coal mine. But he was unaware of the black cloud that was heading towards Senghennydd ...

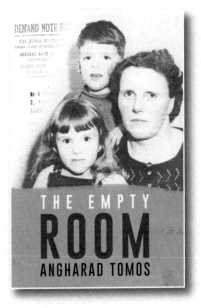

THE EMPTY ROOM
Angharad Tomos

A Welsh family's fight for a basic human right 1952-1960

£5.99

*Shortlisted
for the 2015
Tir na-nOg award
in the original
Welsh*

PAINT!
Angharad Tomos

Why are they painting roadsigns in Wales? Why are they painting the town?

It's the summer of 1969, and a turbulent time in the history of Wales.

£8.50

*Shortlisted
for the 2016
Tir na-nOg award
in the original
Welsh*

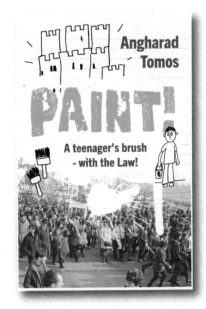

WOVEN
Angharad Tomos

A shocking story of a slave girl in the West Indies and a servant maid in Wales, and the terrible suffering that accompanied slavery.

A historical novel that faces facts and greed and violence ...

£8.50

Shortlisted for the 2021 Tir na-nOg award and Book of the Year in the original Welsh

---

THE IRON DAM
Myrddin ap Dafydd

A novel full of excitement and bravery about ordinary people battling for their area's future.

£5.99

Shortlisted for the 2017 Tir na-nOg award in the original Welsh

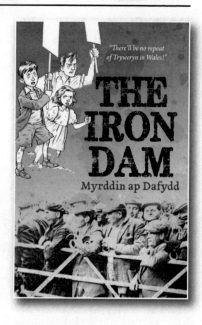

THE MOON IS RED
Myrddin ap Dafydd

Fire at a Bombing School in Llŷn in 1936 and bombs raining down on the city of Gernika in the Basque Country during the Spanish Civil War – and one family's story woven through all of this.

£6.99

Winner of the 2018 Tir na-nOg award in the original Welsh

UNDER THE WELSH NOT
Myrddin ap Dafydd

"you'll get a beating for speaking Welsh ..."

Bob starts at Ysgol y Llan at the end of the summer, but he's worried. He doesn't have a word of English. The 'Welsh Not' stigma for speaking Welsh is still used at that school.

£7.50

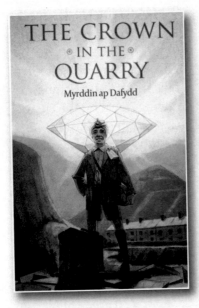

THE CROWN IN THE QUARRY
Myrddin ap Dafydd

The world's largest diamond ... in Blaenau Ffestiniog

The story of evacuees and moving London's treasures to the safety of the quarries during the Second World War.

£7

THE BLACK PIT OF TONYPANDY
Myrddin ap Dafydd

It is 1910, a turbulent time of disputes, strikes and riots in Cwm Rhondda, when the miners are fighting for fair wages and better working conditions.

People from different backgrounds are thrown together, resulting in friendships and conflict ...

£7.99

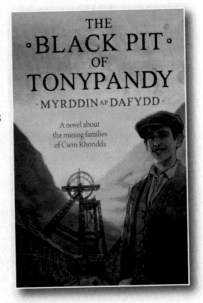

FASTER THAN THE SWORDS
Myrddin ap Dafydd

It's Summer 1843 – the time of the Rebecca Riots. The teenage twins of Tafarn y Wawr in Llangadog find themselves caught up in the struggle and they need to learn from the gypsy Mari Lee how to run faster than the swords ...

£8.50

THE DRAGON IN THE CASTLES
Myrddin ap Dafydd

Discover the adventures of the Castles of Wales

The Holiday Blog twins – Gruff and Gwen – are visiting twenty Welsh castles. They come across strange and exciting stories – histories that are sometimes kept out of sight.

£7.50

WESTERN WILDFIRE
Ifor Wyn Williams

Gruffudd ap Cynan, the fighting flame against the Normans

The story of Gruffudd ap Cynan's fight to regain his kingdom in Gwynedd.

£7.95

THE MAGIC HORNPIPE
Gareth Evans

A gripping story set in Britain, 552 AD, following 12-year old Ina's perilous journey escaping from her enemies. Her only company is Bleiddyn, her wolfdog, and in her bag, the magic hornpipe.

£8.50

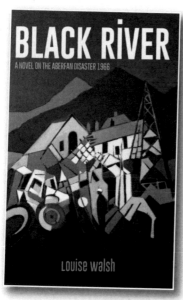

BLACK RIVER
Louise Walsh

(*suitable for Young Adults*)

Harry Roberts is a Cardiff journalist haunted by his failure to cover the Aberfan disaster.

Black River is a powerful piece of investigative drama that draws on the feelings of a wounded nation to show the good and bad of journalists, politicians and villagers alike.

£7.50